"You're going to do *what*?"

Clint asked Pat Garrett later in the saloon.

"I'm going to keep the job," the big man repeated.

"What the hell for?" Clint said. "Look, Gault knew what the story was when he gave you that badge. You don't owe him or this town anything—especially not getting killed for it."

"Look, Clint, if I'm going to be a good lawman, I might as well start now. Would you walk away?"

"I sure as hell would."

"You're a liar. You didn't get your reputation as a good lawman by walking away from trouble," Garrett replied.

"No, but I stayed alive . . ."

Don't miss any of the lusty, hard-riding action in the new Charter Western series, THE GUNSMITH:

And coming next month:

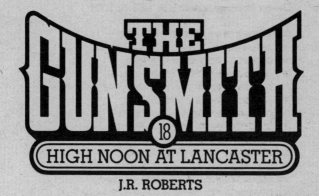

THE GUNSMITH

18

HIGH NOON AT LANCASTER

J.R. ROBERTS

CHARTER BOOKS, NEW YORK

THE GUNSMITH #18: HIGH NOON AT LANCASTER

A Charter Book/published by arrangement with the author

PRINTING HISTORY
Charter Original / July 1983

ISBN: 0-441-30889-9

Charter Books are published by Charter Communications, Inc.,
200 Madison Avenue, New York, New York 10016.
PRINTED IN THE UNITED STATES OF AMERICA

DEDICATION

This one is just
for Christopher

ONE

"That rig looks pretty worn, Jeff," Billy Field said. "What makes you think he's got any money?"

"Look at that horse, stupid," Jeff Wall told his partner. "That's the prettiest piece of horseflesh I've ever seen, bar none."

"Maybe he stole it."

Wall looked at his dim-witted partner and said, "Not everybody steals for a living, Billy."

"Lucky for us," Field said. "If they did there might not be enough to go around."

"Uh, yeah, that's one way to look at it," Wall agreed, to keep his friend happy. In spite of Field's obvious lack of thinking power, Wall liked having him around. Among other things, the kid would shoot anything and anyone Wall aimed him at.

"Let's keep up with him," Wall said, "and wait for a likely spot to ambush him."

"I get to knock him off his seat?" Field asked, fondling his rifle in both hands.

"That's right, Billy," Wall said. "You get to knock the famous Gunsmith off his seat. That'll give you some reputation, kid."

"Yeah," Field said, his eyes lighting up. "I'll be the guy who took the Gunsmith."

Better you than me, Wall thought. *I sure as hell wouldn't want every punk gunman gunning for me.*

"Let's go, Billy," Wall said. "And don't fire a shot until I say so, okay?"

"Sure, Jeff, sure. Like always."

"*Just* like always, Billy boy."

The Gunsmith was too busy thinking about his financial situation to notice the two men who were keeping pace with him from a discreet distance. Cash in hand was getting dangerously low, and if he couldn't find some gunsmithing work in Lancaster it might be time to tap the profits from the Buckskin Saloon, which he had invested in while he was in Brightwater, Arizona some months ago.* His partner, Buckskin Frank Leslie, was depositing his share in a bank here in Texas—that is, if there were any profits.

Clint Adams reined his team in and took out his canteen for a mouthful of water. In another hour or so he'd be in Lancaster, Texas, bellying up to a bar to slake his thirst with a cold beer. Until then, a small mouthful of water now and again would keep the dust from building up to an unbearable degree.

He was to be denied even that small mouthful, however, for as he raised the canteen to his lips a shot rang out and the canteen was thrown from his hands by the force of the bullet that passed through it.

Reacting by instinct, Clint threw himself through the air, following the path of the canteen. A second shot sounded and the bullet struck the wagon where he had been sitting only moments before. Fortunately for him,

---

*The Gunsmith #16: Buckskins and Six-Guns, Charter Books, May, 1983.

it had taken the gunman one shot to find the range, and by that time he was moving.

He struck the ground with his left shoulder and rolled, pulling his gun right-handed at the same time. He kept rolling until he was off the road and into the brush alongside it. Hidden now, he moved to his left as the gunman fired in the area where he had last been seen.

Clint moved into a gulley that ran parallel to the road, and lay there quite still, trying to locate the man who was doing all the shooting. When he was unable to do so, he knew he was going to have to expose himself one more time, but under his conditions, so that he could pinpoint their location.

Before making a move, he was going to have to make the best guess he could at where the shots were coming from. There was only one logical place. About a hundred yards across the road a high bluff rose up steeply, and if a rifleman was sitting up there taking shots at him, *Clint's* handgun wasn't going to do him much good.

He flattened his back against the side of the gulley, held his gun in both hands, took a deep breath and then turned and stood up. Just for something to do he snapped off a useless shot towards the top of the bluff, and then saw the man stand up and aim his rifle at him. He dropped down just as the man fired, and the bullet came very close. Whoever the fellow was, he wasn't a bad shot.

Luckily, he wasn't a great shot, either.

Now he knew where the guy was, but in order to do anything about it, he needed his rifle. For the first time since jumping off his rig he checked to see where it was. The team had kept going until Duke, hitched to the rear, had been able to stop them, but the rig was still a far piece down the road. He could stay under cover most of the way, but in order to get to the rig he was going to have to come out in the open for at least a short time, and the rifleman might just be good enough to pick him off during that time.

Keeping as low as he could, he started following the gulley along the road. He allowed his head to bob into sight from time to time, but apparently the shooter had too much patience to waste his shots. Clint finally reached the point where he was going to have to leave the gulley and cross the road to his rig, leaving himself out in the open long enough for a decent gunman with a repeating rifle to add a couple of pounds of lead to his body weight.

He started up the incline to get back on the road, then stopped and looked at the gun in his hand, where it was about as useful as a finger. He holstered the gun, took a deep breath, and then climbed up onto the road.

Almost immediately he realized that he had been foxed. There wasn't one man with a repeating rifle on that bluff, but two, and suddenly it was hailing lead. He hadn't gone one step when he knew he'd never make it. His hat went flying, the heel of a boot snapped off, and he felt a slug crease his left shoulder. After that, he was back in the gulley, lying on his belly and breathing hard.

He turned over and scrambled for cover so that his back was against the side of the gulley. He touched his fingertips to his left shoulder, and although they came away bloody, there was more blood than damage. He knew, however, that he had just about used up his quota of luck. The next slug that came away wouldn't just take his hat or the heel of his boot; it just might take his life, and he'd become very attached to that.

He didn't pause to ask himself why he was being shot at. The chances were good that it was someone who had recognized him in the town he'd last visited, and decided to go reputation hunting. It had happened before, but if something didn't happen quick—like an earthquake—this would be a very successful attempt.

And the Gunsmith would be very dead.

What happened next wasn't an earthquake, but it was damn near the next thing to a tornado.

Clint became aware of hoofbeats approaching at a gallop and wondered if one of the gunmen was coming down for a closer shot. When the rider came into view he didn't slack his pace and didn't seem to be searching the side of the road for Clint. Whoever he was, he caught the Gunsmith and the two men on the bluff by surprise. It wasn't until he reined in by the rig and Duke that the two riflemen seemed to realize what he was up to, and then it was too late.

The man on the horse pulled Clint's rifle free, jerked his mount around and seemed to know exactly where Clint was. He had started his horse moving again before the riflemen recovered from their surprise and began raining lead down at him.

"Hey, friend!" the man shouted.

"Here!" Clint yelled back.

The man threw Clint's rifle to him, then dove off his horse and into the gulley next to him. The men on the bluff were still firing and both Clint and the stranger began firing back. Suddenly, everything was evened out, and after a few moments the men on the bluff evidently decided they didn't like the shift in the odds.

When the firing from the bluff stopped, Clint and the Samaritan also ceased firing to stop and listen. After a few moments they heard the sounds of horses riding away. Clint was the first to stand up, and the stranger followed, showing himself to be at least four or five inches taller than the Gunsmith.

"Guess they didn't like the odds," the stranger said.

"I wasn't too happy with them either until you showed up," Clint replied.

"Glad I could be of help." The big man stepped easily from the gulley onto the road, then extended a hand to help the Gunsmith up. Clint realized that behind the bushy mustache the man who had saved his bacon couldn't have been more than twenty-five years old.

"Thanks," he said, standing next to the man on the road.

"You okay?" he asked Clint. "You look a little . . . crooked."

"Oh, yeah, I'm fine," Clint answered. "They just creased my shoulder and shot off the heel of my boot," he said, lifting up his left foot as evidence.

"Yeah," the stranger said. "Well, I better chase down my horse. That's a nice black you've got there. Looks like he kept the team from running off."

"Duke, yeah," Clint said. "He's my anchor, all right."

"He's a beauty," the big man said. "Well, let me chase down my nag."

As he started off Clint said, "Hey, wait a minute. You pulled my fat out of the fire and I don't even know your name."

"You going to Lancaster?"

"If that's where the road goes."

"That's where it goes, and I'll probably be there a little later on."

"Great, I'll buy you a drink."

"I'll see you there."

"Yeah," Clint said, as the tall man started off again, "but what's your name?"

"Garrett," the man called out over his shoulder. "Pat Garrett. See you in town, friend!"

TWO

Clint considered going up on the bluff to take a look around, but he decided against it. The bushwhackers might decide to double back and catch him out in the open. He decided just to jump back on his rig and head on into town.

Driving into Lancaster he thought about what to do first: check in at the livery, get his shoulder looked at by a doctor, fix his boot, or just say the hell with it and get a drink.

He decided to take things in order of importance.

"Your shoulder is bleeding, stranger," the bartender said as he set a mug of cold beer down in front of Clint.

"I know," Clint replied, picking up the beer.

"You ought to get that looked at."

Clint drank half the beer and said, "I will, as soon as I finish this beer . . . and take care of my animals."

The liveryman also thought he should tell Clint that he was bleeding, and the Gunsmith promised to have it looked at. He marveled at how concerned the townspeople were about a stranger.

"I'd get them boots fixed too, if I was you," the liveryman added as Clint was leaving. "You could fall and break your neck like that."

"I'll take care of it," Clint promised. "Thanks."

He limped over to the doctor's office on his one boot heel, following the directions given him by the liveryman.

"I'd get that heel fixed if I were you, Mr. Adams," the doctor said while bandaging the shallow crease on his shoulder.

"I intend to," Clint assured him. "There just don't seem to be enough hours in the day to get done all the things you have to get done."

"I know what you mean."

After paying the doctor Clint found a cobbler who was able to make a quick repair on his boot. Then he went back to the livery to pick up his saddlebags and rifle, and got directions from the liveryman to a hotel.

"Ain't but one in town," the man informed him and gave him the directions. As he was leaving the liveryman said, "You're walking a lot better, young fella."

Clint waved his thanks and kept on walking.

He went to the hotel and tried to check in, but when they asked for the money in advance he hesitated.

"Sir," the young clerk asked, "how long will you be staying?"

"I'm not sure," he answered. "Can I pay for one night in advance?"

"One night'll be fine, sir."

He thought about asking how much it would be for a bath, but decided against it. "Can I get a pitcher and basin?"

"Already in the room, sir."

"Okay, thank you."

He went up to the room and stripped off his bloody shirt. He washed himself as best he could with the water in the pitcher, then put on a clean shirt. He counted his money and found that he could probably get himself a meal, some whiskey or a small poker game. He decided to go over to the saloon and see what opportunities presented themselves.

"Got yourself fixed up, I see," the bartender said.

"That's right."

"Another beer?"

"I, uh—"

"Second one's on the house, for a stranger," the man informed him.

"Well, in that case . . ."

He accepted the beer, then turned to take in the room. There were no formal gambling tables, but off in one corner three men were playing poker with silver.

"How much are they playing for?" he asked the bartender.

"Two-bit limit, I think. They don't never play much higher. Looking to make yourself a small stake?"

"I could buy myself a meal," he answered, "but where's the gamble in that, right?"

"I tell you what," the barkeep said. "I like to gamble, but I'm a terrible card player. How much money you got?"

"Not much," Clint said. "About three dollars, give or take two bits."

"I'll match it."

"Why?"

"I'll match it, and we split whatever you win . . . and I'll throw in a sandwich."

"What's your name?" Clint asked him. The bartender was a man of medium height with more than his share of belly. He had a smooth, easy-smiling face, but his gray hair put him at about forty or so.

"Name's Anderson, Charlie Anderson."

"Clint Adams, Charlie, and you've got a deal."

"Here's the money. Take your beer, and I'll bring you over a sandwich."

Clint took the money and approached the three men at the table. "Mind if I sit in?"

"Charlie send you over?" one man asked.

"That's right. Why?"

One of the other men laughed and said, "Charlie's a terrible card player. He's always staking somebody and sending him in against us. You giving him half the profits?"

"That's right," Clint said. "Anybody minds, I'll go my way."

"Hell, mister," the first man said. "We don't mind. Most times the men Charlie backs are worse than him. Set yourself down and let's play cards."

The old chestnut in poker is that it's unlucky to win the first hand, but Clint won that one and just kept on going from there, winning an average of two out of every three hands. It was a combination of his luck and the lackluster play of the other three men. He felt almost guilty taking their money, but losing is a risk everybody takes when they sit down to play poker.

"Well," a player named Andy said after a few hours, "looks like Charlie did himself right proud, this time."

He pushed his chair back, and the other two men followed his move. The game was over.

"That's a considerable amount of our money you got there, friend," the second man said. He answered to the name Red, although there wasn't a red hair on his head. "I hope you'll be in town long enough to give us a chance to get it back."

"I'll be here a few days, at least," he assured them.

"That's fine," Andy said. "Thanks for the game, mister."

"The name's Clint."

"Good night, Clint."

"Good night."

When they left Clint gathered up his winnings and his sandwich plate, and took them and the beer mug back to the bar.

"How'd we do?" Charlie Anderson asked.

"Your share comes to twenty-nine sixty," Clint told him.

"Pass mine over in silver, Clint. You don't want to be jangling so much when you walk."

"I'm much obliged, Charlie," he said.

"I'm the one who's obliged. You're one of the first fellas I've backed who's made me a profit. Be in town long?"

"Few days, maybe."

"Staying at the hotel?"

"It's the only one in town, I hear."

"That's so, but there's a rooming house at the south end of town, run by Mrs. Dean. It's a lot cheaper than the hotel, and it includes meals."

"I'm obliged to you again, Charlie. You make a habit of helping strangers save money?"

"Hey," Charlie said. "I'm just a hell of a guy—and I'm twenty-six bucks and change richer for it."

THREE

Clint spent the night in the hotel, then checked out in the morning and went looking for that boardinghouse. He went to the south end of town, picked out a likely looking structure two stories high, and knocked on the door.

A handsome woman in her early thirties answered. She had short-cropped brown hair, gray eyes, a full figure, and was almost as tall as the Gunsmith.

"Can I help you?" she asked, studying his face.

"Are you Mrs. Dean?"

"I am," she answered. "Laura Dean."

"My name is Clint Adams. I understand you have rooms available."

"That's right. Won't you come in?"

She took him into the living room and offered him tea. When he refused she told him that she would offer him something stronger, but she didn't serve it in the house.

"You can have it in your own room, though, if you like," she added.

"You mean you've decided to accept me as a tenant?"

"You need a place to stay, don't you?" she asked, smiling.

"I wouldn't be here if I didn't."

"There's a bath on the second floor. You can have room number five. The others are all taken."

"I guess that makes me pretty lucky," he commented. "Getting the only room left."

"That depends on how you look at it," she said. "You have the room right next to mine."

He tried to read the look on her face when she said that, but it was unreadable. He thought he detected a little body language, though. Her full breasts seemed to be thrusting themselves towards him, and her hip seemed to be cocked a little bit more, as if she were posing. She didn't have to pose, though, because he could see she was a desirable woman. The tightening in his crotch fully attested to that fact.

"Would you mind if I looked at my room now?"

"Not at all. Have you had breakfast?"

"No, I haven't."

"Well, the others have eaten and gone, but there's some left. I'll have it ready for you when you come down. How do you like your coffee?"

"Black, and strong."

"We've got something in common, then," she said, and left the room, presumably to go into the kitchen. He watched until she disappeared, and then went upstairs.

The room was about the same size as the hotel room, but a damn sight cleaner. The bed was more comfortable, too. Mrs. Dean was apparently an excellent housekeeper.

He dropped off his gear, took a few moments to find where the bath was, then decided to take a quick one when he found some hot water.

When he came down he found the breakfast set out on the table. When she said that there was some left over, he hadn't expected this. There were flapjacks, eggs, potatoes, ham, biscuits and coffee.

"Left over did you say?" he asked, taking a seat.

"There wasn't as much as I thought, so I threw something together," she admitted.

"Mighty nice throwing."

"You bathed," she said. "I thought there might be some hot water left."

"There was just enough. I feel much better."

"I'm sure you'll feel even better after you've eaten."

She started back to the kitchen and he said, "Aren't you going to eat?"

"I've already eaten," she said. "Now I've got to clean the kitchen. I'll join you for a cup of coffee when I'm finished, though, and we can get to know one another a little better. I like to know something about my tenants."

"That's fine with me. I haven't had a conversation with a lovely lady in quite some time."

"Oh, Mr. Adams," she said, sounding as if she were chiding him, but she didn't elaborate on just how she had meant it. She went into the kitchen and he began to eat and didn't stop until there was nothing left.

When she came out she looked surprised and said, "You must have been starved."

"Pretty near," he said. "All I had last night was a saloon sandwich."

"Would you like some more?"

"No, no, this was plenty . . . and it was delicious. Would you like that cup of coffee, now?"

"Thank you, yes."

She sat down and he poured her a cup.

"Thank you, Mr. Adams. It's been a long time since

someone has poured for me."

"Well, then, I guess that makes us friends, doesn't it?"

She laughed and said, "I guess it does."

"That means you'll have to call me Clint."

"And you'll have to call me Laura," she said. "And I think we are going to be very good friends, Clint."

"No games, Laura?"

She shook her head, holding his eyes and said boldly, "No games between us, Clint."

FOUR

They went to her room, which she said was the largest in the house. She had a big brass bed with a mattress that was twice as thick as the one in his room—four times as thick as the one he'd slept on the night before.

Before undressing she drew the curtains across the window.

"Making love with the sun shining through the window is so sinful," she said. "Don't you think?"

"I don't think there's anything sinful about a man and a woman being together, no matter what the time of day is."

"That's a nice thought," she said. She walked up to him, put her hands on his shoulders and kissed him. It started out slow, but developed into a long, lingering kiss. "And that was nice too."

"Very nice."

"You know, if you take your boots off, I think I'll be almost as tall as you."

"Let's see."

He sat down on the bed and started taking his boots off, and then she helped him. When they were off they both stood up and found that she was still a couple of inches short of his height.

"That's all right," she said, unbuttoning his shirt and sliding her hands inside and around him. "I don't mind."

"Neither do I," he agreed. He encircled her with his arms and they kissed again, slowly and sweetly.

"Um," she said, drawing back and taking a deep breath. "I'm feeling a little funny, here." She placed a hand between her breasts.

"How funny?"

"Well, I'm a widow, you know."

"I know," he said, kissing her neck. She smelled so clean and natural.

"So I'm not a virgin."

"Of course not."

"And since my husband's death five years ago, I haven't exactly been celibate."

"Of course not," he said, unbuttoning her dress.

"But something is happening here . . ."

"It certainly is," he said, pulling her dress down over her shoulders.

"Oh, God," she said, as he undressed her completely and ran the palms of his hands over the nipples of her full breasts. She closed her eyes and arched her back as he ran his lips down her neck, over her shoulders, and then began to circle her nipples with his tongue without actually touching them.

"Oh, God," she said again, unbuttoning his shirt the rest of the way and helping him out of it. She ran her hands over his back and shoulders, then moved them between them and began to undo his pants.

"Take them off," she said urgently. "Take them off."

She pushed him back to the bed, and then down on it, tugging his trousers off, and then practically stripping him of his underwear.

"There," she said. She climbed aboard him, straddling him on her knees, and began to run her hands over his chest. At the same time, he reached up and began to tweak her distended nipples.

She was sitting on his rigid penis so that it was flattened against his belly, and now she started rubbing her damp thatch up and down the length of it.

"Oh, does that feel good," he told her.

"Oh?" she said. She leaned down and began to tongue his nipples while continuing to massage his penis in long, even strokes.

"Oh, yes," he breathed. Reaching down he took hold of her hips and slid her high enough so that he could prod her portal and slide right into her.

"Now *that*," she said, nibbling on his ear lobe, "feels divine."

Now that he was firmly inside her, she began riding him up and down violently with her hands braced against his chest. He continued to play with her breasts, working to control his urge to come and wait for her—although she wasn't making it easy. She kept running her tongue over her full lips, as if she were savoring her own taste, and that simple act was fanning his excitement.

He tightened his grip on her hips in an effort to slow down her churning movements, but at that very moment she started to babble, "Oh God, here it comes, I feel it, here it comes, it's coming. Oh shit, it's coming . . ."

Suddenly she jammed her crotch down flat against his and began to grind herself against him, and he released the hold he had on himself and began to spurt into her, filling her with his seed. She began to scrape his chest with her nails, leaving two red lines, one above and one below his right nipple.

"Oh, Clint," she said when her tremors had ceased, "look what I did."

"What?" he asked, looking down at his chest.

"I marked you."

He watched as she ran the same two fingers that did the damage over the scratches.

"So you did."

She wiggled her hips and then widened her eyes saying, "My God, you're still hard, aren't you?"

"I guess so," he said, sliding his hands over the smooth globes of her behind. "You want to try for matching scratches on the other side?"

FIVE

Firmly entrenched as a resident of Laura Dean's rooming house, Clint left her to freshen up and made a belated visit to the town sheriff. It was a practice he maintained in every town he visited, announcing his arrival to the local law. Lawmen didn't like it when men with reputations came to town unannounced. Sometimes they thought somebody was trying to sneak by them.

At the sheriff's office he entered without knocking. The chest of the man sitting behind the desk was possibly the most disappointing place he had ever seen a sheriff's badge pinned.

The man had a long, angular, unshaven jaw and red-rimmed eyes. His left hand was resting on top of the desk, and his right was resting on the neck of a whiskey bottle.

"Are you the sheriff?"

"That's right," the man said, tapping the badge. "Sheriff."

"My name is Clint Adams, Sheriff," Clint said, approaching the desk. The sheriff could have been anywhere from thirty to forty years old. In his condition it was hard to tell.

"So?"

"I've just arrived in town and I just wanted to check in with you."

"Why? You wanted?"

"No."

"Wouldn't matter if you was," the sheriff said, and proceeded to suck liquid from the bottle.

"I think there's an incident I should tell you about, Sheriff," Clint said, although he was dubious about the wisdom of his own words.

"Why?"

"Because you're the sheriff."

"Not after today."

"Why not?"

"They're taking my tin away."

And not a moment too soon, Clint thought.

"Who will the new sheriff be?"

"I don't know and I don't care," he said. "Now would you mind leaving? I'm saying good-bye to my office." He tipped the neck of the bottle toward the door, then back toward his mouth, where it found a home.

"Enjoy yourself."

Clint left the office and headed for the saloon.

"Good morning," Charlie Anderson greeted him. "My gold mine."

"Is it too early for a beer?"

"Not for you. Belly up."

"Thanks."

When Charlie brought his beer Clint said, "I just came from the sheriff's office."

"You're kidding," Charlie said. "Why? That drunk lock you up for being drunk?"

"I understand that starting tomorrow you won't have a sheriff."

"Looks that way. You interested?"

"Oh, no, not me."

Charlie frowned knowingly and said, "You sound

like you're speaking from experience—*bad* experience.''

"Some good, some bad," Clint said, "but all past, and I want to keep it that way."

"I don't know," Charlie said. "Even with your heart only half in it you'd have to do a better job than Art Block."

"How long was he sheriff?"

"Couple of months."

"Who was sheriff before then?"

"We had a good one for three years," Charlie said. "Ed Samuels, a really good man. Oh, he wasn't a great hand with a gun, and he wasn't much in a fight. Ed was almost sixty, but he knew how to do his job."

"What happened?"

"Heart attack, right here in the saloon. He was dead before he hit the floor."

"That's a shame."

"Sure was. Nobody wanted the job except Art Block, and the town council agreed to appoint him to finish out Ed's term."

"Which was?"

"Five more months, only after two the town council got tired of watching their sheriff lock himself up every night for being drunk."

"Isn't there a deputy?"

"No need for one, really," Charlie said. "And the council likes to save money."

"Like any town, no matter what the size."

"Don't like town councils, huh?"

"Not much," Clint said, which was an understatement. They had given him more grief during the years he'd spent as a lawman, and were a big reason he had chucked it all in.

"I don't blame you. As a business owner, I've been

on the council of this town for five years, and it's no fun from my end, either.''

"I can imagine.''

''Are you sure you wouldn't like to take the job on just for the remaining three months of Ed Samuels's term?''

"What makes you think I'd qualify for the job?'' Clint asked.

"Come on, Clint, I recognized the name. If you don't qualify, who does?''

"Sorry, Charlie, but no deal.''

"Okay. You must have your reasons.''

"Believe me, I do.''

"Another beer?''

"Sure,'' Clint said, "why not start the day right?''

"How'd you like the widow?''

"Handsome woman.''

"And then some,'' Charlie added, raising his eyebrows.

"Did you know her husband?''

The bartender shook his head, saying, "She didn't live here while she was married. Moved here after her husband's death.''

"I see.''

"I've heard she's a great cook.''

"That would be an understatement.''

"She cook for you already?''

"Breakfast.''

"You must have impressed her.''

"Believe me,'' Clint said, rubbing his hand over the right side of his chest, "she made quite an impression on me too.''

SIX

Before leaving the saloon, Clint made sure that Charlie knew that he was in the gunsmithing business—information to which the bartender raised an ironic eyebrow—and that he'd appreciate the man referring business to him. Within an hour he had customers showing up at his wagon in the livery, and he had enough work to keep him busy most of the afternoon, and to make him a little more money.

He was working on an old Navy Colt that needed a thorough cleaning and a new firing pin when someone banged on the side of his wagon.

"I'll be out in a moment," he shouted.

"I hear you fix guns," a man's voice called.

"That's right," Clint said, climbing out of the wagon. When he turned around he found himself face to face with young and tall Pat Garrett.

"Hello."

"I thought the wagon looked familiar," Garrett said. "How are you?"

"Alive, thanks to you. What can I do for you?"

Garrett handed Clint a Colt. 45 and said, "It's misfiring almost every other time I pull the trigger."

"I'll fix it," Clint said, taking it from him. "No charge."

"Whoa, no way," the younger man said. "This here's your living. I'll pay for it."

"All right, but you've got to let me buy you that drink."

"Fine. I've got to see somebody, but I should be over at the saloon in about thirty minutes."

"Okay. I'll have your gun ready."

"That fast?"

"That fast."

"Well," Pat Garrett said, "I heard you were fast."

Pat Garrett left the Gunsmith's wagon and walked over to the office of the Mayor of Lancaster, William C. Gault, a dime novelist who had come from the East years ago to have someplace quiet to write his stories. He had become a well-liked figure in the town, and had been elected mayor. He was serving his third successive term at the age of—well, over sixty. Mayor Gault never let on about his true age. He felt that admitting that he was only five foot two inches tall was painful enough.

"Mayor Gault, my name is Pat Garrett."

"You're a big fella, ain't you?" Gault asked from behind his desk. "How tall are you? I'll bet you're a hell of a lot taller than five foot two."

"Yes, sir."

"What can I do for you, Mr. Garrett? Do you live in town?"

"Outside of town, sir. I work on the Millar place."

"Ken Millar," Gault said. "Ken's a good friend of mine."

"I know that, sir. He told me to tell you that I had his backing in this."

"In what?"

"I'd like the job as sheriff."

"Sheriff?" Gault asked. "Aren't you a little young?"

"Yes, sir," Garrett said. "But I've got something that Ed Samuels and Art Block don't."

"What's that?"

"I'm alive, and I'm sober."

"So you are, lad," Gault said. "So you are."

Clint got to the saloon first, carrying Garrett's gun tucked into his belt.

"I been sending some business your way," Charlie Anderson said when he walked in.

"So I noticed," Clint said. "Paying customers too." He slapped the price of two beers on the bar and said, "Let me buy you a drink."

"You got it."

"I'm waiting for somebody else to show up, so I can buy him a drink too."

"Who's that?"

"Young fella name of Pat Garrett."

"I know Pat," Charlie said. "He works as a hand on the Millar ranch. Where'd you meet him?"

"On the road to town yesterday. A couple of reputation seekers pinned me down and he pulled my bacon out of the fire. I think that's worth a drink, don't you?"

"At least one," Charlie agreed.

Clint drank half of his beer and then said, "So tell me, who has the council been considering for the job of sheriff?"

"We've thrown so many names around I've lost count," Charlie said. "It'll all boil down to who Mayor Gault wants." Charlie went on to explain the mayor's story.

"Dime novels, huh? I don't read them."

"He's done some stuff on Bill Hickok, Ben Thompson—say, you wouldn't have known those fellas, would you?"

"Both of them," Clint said.

"Hey, maybe the mayor would like to do something on you," Charlie suggested.

"Forget it."

"No, think about it, Clint—"

"I said forget it," the Gunsmith snapped. "I've got enough problems as it is without some writer making me bigger than life."

"My friend, where have you been?" Charlie asked. "The Gunsmith is already twice as big as life."

"Yeah," Clint said, finishing his beer. "Give me another drink, will you, only make it whiskey this time."

"Sure."

At that moment the batwing doors swung inward and Pat Garrett seemed to fill the room.

"There's your guest," Charlie said.

"Well, young Mr. Garrett," Clint said as Garrett approached the bar. "What will you have?"

"Whiskey."

"On me," Clint reminded Charlie, who proceeded to pour two drinks.

"Here's to the man who saved my hide," Clint said, raising his glass.

They drank, and Garrett said, "Now it's my turn to buy. I've got something to celebrate."

As Charlie poured, he said, "What's the celebration about, kid?"

Garrett picked up his glass and said, "Here's to my new job."

"What's the new job?" Clint asked.

"Gentlemen," Garrett said proudly, "you are looking at the new sheriff of Lancaster, Texas."

SEVEN

"What do you know about being a lawman?" Charlie Anderson asked Pat Garrett.

Garrett looked at Clint and said, "That's what I wanted to talk to you about."

"Me?" Clint said. He looked at Charlie, who gave him a knowing look.

"Could we sit down and talk?" Garrett asked.

"Sure, Pat," Clint said.

"Give me a bottle, will you, Charlie?" Garrett asked. He accepted a bottle from the bartender and he and Clint walked to a corner table. Clint took the chair facing the door, with his back to the wall, and Garrett sat across from him, with his back to the door.

"What can I do for you, Pat?"

"Be my deputy."

Clint hesitated a moment, then said, "Sorry, no way—"

"I recognized your name when I heard it, Clint."

"That happens on occasion."

"The Gunsmith could teach me a lot about being a lawman."

"I won't wear a star, Pat."

"You want to pay me back for yesterday?" Garrett asked him.

"Of course, but—"

"Then teach me what I need to know to be a good lawman. It's what I want to do with the rest of my life, Clint, and I want to do it right."

Knowing that he was honor bound to repay his debt to Pat Garrett and couldn't refuse him in good conscience, Clint poured himself another drink and tried to think of a way of keeping the task from being a distasteful one.

"All right, Pat, I'll make a deal with you," he finally said.

"What?"

"I'll stay around and get you started on the right track, but I won't wear a star." Garrett was silent. "Take it or leave it."

"I'll take it," Garrett said. "Let's have another drink on it."

"As soon as you change your seat."

"My seat? Why?"

"Because the first thing you have to learn as a lawman is to keep your eyes open for trouble."

"So?"

Pointing with the index finger of his right hand Clint said, "Trouble usually comes in the front door. If it did that now, it would be staring you right in the back."

Garrett thought about it a moment, then moved his shoulders uncomfortably and said, "I think I see what you mean."

He got up and moved to the chair at his right, then angled it so that he could see the front door.

"Okay," Clint said. "Now down that drink and then stick to beer."

"Why?"

"Because if trouble comes in you want to be able to see it, and not through a drunken haze."

"Gotcha," Garrett said. He finished the drink he'd poured, then picked up the bottle and put it on the table next to him. "On me," he told the men seated there. "Compliments of the new sheriff," Garrett added, then got up to go to the bar and get a couple of beers.

The two men at the next table stared at his back strangely while the Gunsmith studied them. When one of them saw Clint watching them, he nudged the other one and both of them got up and left.

When Garrett came back with the beers Clint said, "You've got a lot to learn, kid. An awful lot."

"What did I do now?" Garrett asked, looking puzzled. "The beer's cold." He looked around and said, "What happened to those two? Didn't they like my whiskey?"

"Your whiskey was fine; it's your job they didn't like."

"It ain't even mine yet—not until tomorrow."

"Well, then, don't be walking around telling people you're the new sheriff. You're liable to get a bullet in the back before you even pin on your star."

"I guess I do have a lot to learn."

"Yeah," Clint said. "And I'm going to have to stay around and teach you, because I'd never forgive myself if I left and you got yourself killed."

Garrett smiled and now that Clint had gotten to know him a bit he looked more like what he really was, a youngster whose body had grown faster than his head. He was approaching the job of sheriff with way too much boyish enthusiasm. His size would probably prevent him from being challenged by any drunks to fist fights and such, but when serious trouble arose, he was going to have to be able to approach it seriously.

That would have to be the first thing he learned, and learned well.

EIGHT

The next morning Garrett called for Clint at the rooming house—rousted him out of Laura Dean's bed, in fact—to go over to the mayor's office with him.

At the sound of the pounding on the door Laura had slid out of bed and into a robe and gone down to answer the door.

"It's a man named Pat Garrett," she told Clint when she returned, "and he's about nine feet tall."

"Christ!"

"What does he want, Clint?" she asked, looking amused.

"He wants me to teach him how to be a lawman," Clint said, looking around for his pants.

"What?"

"He's the new sheriff."

"He's a little young, isn't he?"

"That's okay," he said, pulling his pants on. "What he lacks in years he makes up for in inches."

"Really?"

"You have a filthy mind, woman."

He finished getting dressed and asked, "It safe for me to leave?"

"The others are either still in their rooms, or have

34

already left," she said. "I guess you'll miss breakfast."

"I'll be back for leftovers."

"I'll be waiting."

He slipped out of her room unseen and found Garrett waiting in the living room.

"Good morning," Garrett said. "Ready?"

"For what, lesson one?"

"I have to go be sworn in," the younger man said, "and I thought you'd like to be my witness."

"I was hoping you'd ask," Clint said. "Lead on."

They walked over to Mayor Gault's office and Clint asked, "Will the old man be in this early?"

"I understand he's usually in his office by seven, working on a story."

"Wonderful," Clint said. "Maybe we'll get to read chapter one."

On the way in they passed Art Block, who was leaving—without the badge.

"Which one of you is taking my job?" he asked.

"The big one," Clint said.

"I hope you're ready for the Chamberses shavetail," Block said to Garrett.

"Chamberses?" Clint asked as Block staggered away. "Who are they?"

"I'm not sure," Garrett said. "But the name sounds familiar. Come on, let's go inside."

Gault was standing when they entered his office, and he extended his hand to Garrett and said, "Welcome, Sheriff."

"Thank you, Mayor."

"And who is this with you?" Gault asked. "Have you chosen a deputy already?"

"This is Clint Adams, Mayor."

"Adams?" Gault said. "I know that name. The Gunsmith, right?"

"That's right, sir," Garrett said before Clint had a chance to speak.

"Well, well, this is indeed a pleasure, Mr. Adams. I've heard a lot about you."

Clint simply nodded and gave the little man a wan smile, but Gault was not content to stop there.

"I don't know if you're aware of the fact that I'm a writer as well as mayor of Lancaster."

"I, uh, had heard something about that, Mayor."

"We should get together and talk. I understand you were a good friend of ole Jim Hickok."

"That's right."

"I've done several stories about Wild Bill, and they were all well received back East. Perhaps we could talk some about your own exploits."

"I doubt that, sir."

"Huh?" the mayor replied, looking puzzled.

"Sir, could we get on with the swearing in?" Garrett asked. "I'm anxious to get started."

"Oh, of course, lad." Gault reached down and picked up the sheriff's badge from his desk. "Here you go lad. Wear it in good health."

"Uh, is that it, sir?" Garrett asked.

"It's only temporary, lad," Gault said. "Unless you decide to run formally three months from now."

"I probably will, sir."

"Well, if that's the case, lad, you better start campaigning now." Gault turned to Clint and said, "Now about that talk—"

"Maybe another time, Mayor," Clint said, grabbing Garrett's elbow. "We'd better go check out your office, Sheriff."

"Uh, right," Garrett said, looking at the badge in his hand.

"We'll get together later today," Gault called out to Clint.

"Sure, Mayor. My pleasure."

They were almost out the door when Gault said, "Oh, Sheriff. Before you leave there's something you should be aware of."

"What's that, sir?"

Gault seated himself behind his desk and said, "Well, I've received some rather disturbing news. It seems that Willy Chambers and his brothers have let it be known that they are on their way to Lancaster to, uh, burn it to the ground."

"Chambers?" Clint said, recalling what Block had said.

"The Chambers gang, to be precise," Gault said.

"A gang," Clint repeated. "Who brought you this news, Mayor?"

"Ex-sheriff Block, just a few moments ago."

"And how did he find out about it?"

"A telegram that he got yesterday," Gault said, holding up the flimsy in his hand.

"Mayor Gault," Clint said, walking back to the man's desk, "were you taking Block's badge away, or was he giving it up?"

"Well, actually we were going to take it away from him, but he came in yesterday and said that it was his last day on the job. In fact, he's leaving town today."

"Come on, kid," Clint said, heading for the door.

"Where?"

"To talk to Art Block before he gets away. You've been suckered!"

"What about that talk?" Gault called out.

"Later!"

Outside Garrett said, "Where are we going?"

"To the livery stable. We've got to grab Block before he leaves town."

Garrett was off at a run once he knew where they were going, and got there first. When Clint arrived, he found Art Block dangling from the hands of Pat Garrett.

"Tell him to put me down!" Block shouted.

"I can't do that, Art," Clint said, stopping to catch his breath. "He's the sheriff, now."

"Jesus," Block said. "Okay, what do you want?"

Garrett looked at Clint for the answer, and the Gunsmith nodded for the lawman to put Block on his feet.

"I want to know about the Chambers gang, Block," Clint said as the ex-lawman backed away from Pat Garrett.

"What about them?"

"When are they coming, why, the whole story. Give."

"I got a friend in New Mexico who sent me the message that they were on their way. They should be here in a few days."

"Why?"

"They were born here, and after they left, Dan Chambers, the old man, became the town drunk and eventually died."

"And the sons hold that against the town?"

"Yeah, Willy does. He's the oldest. He's been rounding up his brothers, and when he finally got them all together they started for Lancaster."

"How many of them are there?"

"There's four brothers, but the gang's got about nine or ten men, in all."

"That's great," Clint said. He looked at Pat Garrett and said, "You've been set up, kid."

"He wanted to be sheriff," Block said.

"And you don't anymore," Clint said. "But why leave town?"

"They're gonna level this town out, friend, and I don't want to be here when they do."

Clint hesitated a moment, then said, "Okay, Art, you can go."

Block sprinted for his horse and climbed aboard. Clint turned to leave the livery and Garrett followed.

Outside, Block wheeled his horse around to face them and said, "Hey, kid, there's something else you should know."

"What?" Garrett said.

"Willy's old man died in jail," Block said, "and when he and his brothers get here, that's where they're gonna start." He gave Garrett a small salute and said, "Good luck, Sheriff. You're gonna need it."

NINE

"You're going to do *what*?" Clint asked Pat Garrett later in the saloon.

"I'm going to keep the job," the big man repeated.

"What the hell for?" Clint said. "Look, Gault knew what the story was when he gave you that badge. You don't owe him or this town anything—especially not getting killed for it."

"Look, Clint, if I'm going to be a good lawman, I might as well start now. Would you walk away?"

"I sure as hell would."

"You're a liar. You didn't get your reputation as a good lawman by walking away from trouble."

"No, but I stayed alive by doing it."

Garrett shook his head slowly and said, "You can leave, Clint. I won't hold you to your promise. Not under these conditions."

"And what are you going to do? Face the Chambers gang by yourself?"

"I'll get some help."

"From where?"

"The townspeople, the ranchers—"

"I've been through this, Pat. You're not going to find as much help as you think."

"I'll take what I can get."

"Jesus, you're stubborn!"

"I guess it takes a little of that too, to make a good lawman, right?"

"You've got more than enough."

"Don't worry about me, Clint," Garrett said, standing up. "I appreciate the fact that you were ready to help, and—"

"Sit down, sit down," Clint said. "I'm not going anywhere."

"I've got to go and—"

"Don't be in such a hurry to play target, Pat," Clint said, grabbing his arm and pulling him back into his seat. "Have another beer."

Clint waved at Charlie Anderson, who nodded and brought over two beers.

"Is it true?" he asked.

"Is what true?" Clint said.

"That the Chambers gang is on its way to town?"

"How did you hear that?"

"Art Block told Henry, the liveryman, and he's been spreading it all over town."

"Yes, it's true," Garrett told Charlie, "and I'm going to need some volunteer deputies, Charlie."

"Well, you've got me," Charlie said, "and that makes two of us. Good luck finding anyone else."

"You two don't seem to have much faith in the townspeople," Pat Garrett said. "This is their home, you know. They're not just going to let some gang ride in and burn it to the ground."

"Starting with the jail," Charlie reminded him.

Garrett ignored the remark and stood up, towering over both men.

"I've got to get started looking for deputies," the new sheriff said. "I'll see you both later."

Holding his back stiff, Garrett marched out of the saloon to look for his deputies, leaving the two men behind him shaking their heads.

"That badge has gone to his head already," Charlie said, sitting down with Clint and curling his hand around Garrett's untouched beer.

"No, that's not it," Clint said. "The kid really wants to be a good lawman, Charlie."

"He's young."

"He reminds me of me when I was young."

"You would have stayed and faced a whole gang without any help?" Charlie asked.

"I would be doing the same thing he's doing," Clint said. "Will you really stand with him?"

"Sure," Charlie said, then added, "right next to the Gunsmith."

Clint grinned and patted the man on the shoulder. "You're right, Charlie. We'll both be there, but we've also got to do what we can to get our new sheriff some more help. What ranch was it that he worked on again?"

"The Millar place. It's about five miles north of town. Biggest spread in the area."

"Lots of hands?"

"Twenty or thirty, I'd say."

"I don't think he'll go out there first," Clint said. "He'd be too proud to ask Millar for help unless he absolutely had to. He'll check around town first," he added, standing up.

"And you?"

"I'll go out and talk to Millar. Maybe he can get some of his men to volunteer. See what you can do with the men who come in here, Charlie."

"Sure thing, Clint," the bartender said. "I'll get them drunk, and sign them up."

"That wasn't exactly what I had in mind," Clint said, "but work on it."

TEN

Clint saddled Duke and rode him north to the Millar ranch, the Bar M. He was impressed with the size of the spread, and equally impressed by the fact that Ken Millar had not gone overboard on the size of his house. Most big ranchers seemed to think that having a large spread meant having a large house, to show how well off they were.

He rode up to the front of the house where he was greeted by a rangy looking fella with blond hair and jug-handle ears.

"Can I help you, stranger?"

"I'd like to see Mr. Millar."

"We're not hiring, if you're looking for a job," the man informed him.

"That's not why I'm here."

"Kin I tell the boss why you are here?"

"Tell him it's about Pat Garrett."

"Anything happen to Pat?"

"No," Clint answered, and then added to himself, *Not yet*. "I'd just like to talk about him."

"Well, step down, then. If it's about Pat, the boss'll want to see you. He's sure fond of that boy."

Clint dismounted and the man said, "I'll have someone take care of that animal, friend. In fact, I'll have a guard put on him."

"Thanks."

"Knock on the door and tell the little filly who answers that Jug sent you."

"You'd be Jug."

"Is that a guess?" the man asked, laughing and fingering one ear.

Clint laughed with him, then mounted the steps and knocked on the door.

The filly who answered wasn't quite as little as he had expected from what Jug said. She was blond, about seventeen, with pert little breasts that pushed out against the front of her simple frock. She was cute, with a pug nose and freckles, but her blossoming body belied the innocent face.

"Can I help you?" she asked.

"Jug sent me. I'd like to talk to Mr. Millar about Pat Garrett."

"Is Pat all right?" she asked, anxiously.

"Yes, ma'am, he's just fine. I'd just like to talk about him."

"I'll tell my uncle," she said. She started away from the door, then stopped and asked, "What's your name?"

"Clint Adams. I'm staying in town."

"You might as well come in and wait in the parlor."

She left him waiting and went to find her uncle. She soon returned with a tall man with graying hair and a white mustache.

"Mr. Adams? I'm Ken Millar."

He extended a work-roughened hand to Clint and they shook hands.

"I understand you want to talk about Pat Garrett."

"Yes, sir. I'll try not to take too much of your time."

"Don't worry about that," he said. "I'm quite fond of Pat. I'm sorry he left me, but I think it was commendable for him to want to become a lawman. I supported him with Mayor Gault, and I'll support him if he decides to run for election in three months."

"He may not have three months, sir."

"What do you mean?"

Clint looked at the girl, who returned his gaze boldly, tilting her chin up.

"Donna, why don't you go and get us some coffee?"

"I want to hear about Pat, Uncle."

"And I want some coffee. Scat."

"Drat," she said. She turned and stalked from the room.

"My sister's daughter," he explained. "Her parents are both dead."

"I see."

"Please, sit down and tell me what's happening with Pat."

"I'm sure you know that he did get the job as sheriff."

"I had an idea. I had already spoken to Bill Gault about it, and he agreed to give Pat the job."

"I guess you figured you were doing Pat a favor."

Millar frowned and said, "You sound as if you don't think I did."

"I'll let you be the judge," Clint said, and went on to explain about the Chambers gang.

The rancher took a few moments to light a pipe and reflect on what he'd been told, then stood up just as Donna Millar came into the room carrying a tray of coffee and cups.

"How do you like your coffee, Mr. Adams?" she asked politely.

"Black, thanks."

She poured and handed him the cup, prepared her uncle's and handed it to him.

"Scat, kitten," he told her. She pouted, but obeyed.

"Cute," Clint said.

"Favors her mother," Millar said. "This is disturbing news you've brought me, Mr. Adams."

"I'm sorry."

"And I'm afraid you might be right. I may not have done Pat such a great favor. I'll talk to him about giving up the job."

"I've only recently met him, sir, but I've seen his stubborn streak."

"Yes, you're right about that. What else can we do?"

"To face the gang he's going to need help, Mr. Millar, and lots of it. Do you think any of your men would volunteer as special deputies?"

"I'm sure they would, if Pat asked."

"If he doesn't have any luck in town—and I don't think he will—I think he will come out here." Clint stood up and said, "When he does, Mr. Millar, I'd appreciate it if you didn't tell him that I'd been here. You understand."

They shook hands again and the rancher said, "Knowing Pat, yes, I do understand."

Millar walked Clint to the front door.

"You seem to have become pretty attached to Pat Garrett yourself, Mr. Adams."

"He reminds me a lot of myself, when I was his age."

"That's funny. I've always felt that way too. Thanks for coming out, Mr. Adams. I'm sure we'll be seeing each other again."

"Thank you, sir."

Clint descended the steps and Jug brought Duke over.

"Horse is a little ornery, isn't he?" Jug asked.

"Only to strangers."

"A one-man horse, huh?"

"Yep."

Clint mounted up and Jug asked, "Any luck with the old man?"

"We got alone fine."

"I'm the foreman you know. If there's any kind of problem—"

"No problem, Jug. Thanks for taking care of my horse."

"Sure, any time."

Clint rode away from the Bar M with a good feeling about Ken Millar. He was sure that if Pat came to the rancher for help, he'd get all he could use.

So much for first impressions.

Clint was halfway back to town when he heard the shot and thought, *Not again*.

He launched himself from Duke's back, landed rolling and came to a stop with his gun out behind a boulder. When there were no further shots and he was sure that there would not be, he called Duke back, remounted and rode back to town, deep in thought, but still aware for further attempts.

This was the second time in three days that someone had taken a shot at him, and that was too much, even for the Gunsmith.

ELEVEN

Jeff Wall put up his hand to signal his partner, Billy Field, to rein in his horse. Wall figured that they had gone far enough away to make sure that the Gunsmith wasn't following them.

"That's the second time you missed, Billy boy," Wall said to his partner. "You must be slipping."

"I'll get him next time," Field promised. "Wait and see! You should have let me take him in the saloon, Jeff, when we found out who he was."

"Are you kidding?" Wall asked. "Now that we do know who he is, *this* is the only way to take him."

"I'm faster than him."

"Sure, Billy, sure," Wall said. "But we'll do it my way. Come on, let's go."

"Where?"

"Well, the word around Lancaster is that the Chambers gang is on its way to Lancaster, coming from New Mexico."

"So?"

"So maybe they need a couple of extra guns," Wall suggested. "There's safety in numbers, my friend."

"Huh?"

Wall laughed, shook his head and said, "Just follow me, Billy boy."

"Just like always," Field said.

"That's right, Billy, *just* like always."

Willy Chambers had visions of himself as the new Jesse James, but the plain fact of the matter was that the Chambers gang did not even come close to measuring up to the James Gang.

Nobody ever had the nerve to tell Willy that to his face, though. Willy Chambers wasn't a big man, physically, but what he lacked in size he made up for with pure meanness. Even his brothers—all younger than Willy—were afraid of him.

"This is crazy," Matt, the youngest brother, said.

"What is?" Rob Chambers asked. He was the second oldest, after Willy.

"Going back to Lancaster," Matt said. "I don't even want to smell that town again."

"Yeah, well, when we're done with it, there won't be nothing to smell but smoke," Seth Chambers said.

"It's still crazy," Matt said. "Ain't no reason for it."

"So go and tell Willy," Seth said. "He thinks that Pa is enough of a reason."

Matt Chambers made a noise with his mouth and said, "Worthless old drunk."

"Tell *that* to Willy," Seth told him.

The Chambers gang was camped ten miles from the border between New Mexico and Texas, on the New Mexico side. In addition to the four brothers, there were seven other members of the gang, all professional bank and train robbers, all fairly proficient with their guns—except for one man. John Stud.

Stud was not merely proficient, he was expert, and as expert as you could get. Willy Chambers maintained that Stud was the best man he'd ever seen with a gun—other than himself. The other men in the gang, however, including the brothers, knew that Stud was a better man than Willy with a gun.

If Willy Chambers was not as good with a gun as he thought, he did have one thing going for him, and that was his brains. He had been smart enough to successfully guide the gang through almost every job that he planned. His shortcomings in that area were that he often set his sights too low, settling for jobs that were too small to gain the gang the notoriety of the Jameses or the Youngers.

Still, no one member of the gang was man enough to stand up to Willy—except perhaps John Stud, who had no desire to. He enjoyed doing what he did and did not have aspirations to being the leader of any gang. Let someone else do the thinking, he would happily do the killing.

Stud was not a big man, and his hands were especially small, although there was no shortage of strength there. He attributed his ability to draw and fire so quickly to the size of his hands, coupled with the strength of his fingers. Big men often had hands too large to allow them to handle a gun well, unless it was a very large gun, and then you started to have problems with the weight of the weapon.

Stud did not have to deal with any of those problems. There was nothing in the way of drawing and firing his weapon with amazing speed and accuracy. He only hoped that when they arrived in Lancaster there would be someone there to give him a little competition. He liked nothing better than outdrawing and killing a man who was himself fast and skillful.

This was John Stud's reason for living—which

could have meant that, if and when he got to Lancaster
and discovered the Gunsmith there, he'd be in for the
thrill of his life.

TWELVE

Clint got back to town just in time for dinner at Laura Dean's boardinghouse. When he entered she came out to meet him and said, "I was afraid you wouldn't be in time. Dinner should be ready in about fifteen minutes."

"I'm just going to clean up," he told her, touching her arm.

"All right," she said, smiling at him, and he thought he could detect a shine in her eyes. It was the kind of a shine a woman usually gets when she thinks she's found her man, and Clint did not want to get into that situation with Laura Dean. He made a mental note to take it up with her honestly in the near future.

He gave her arm a pat, smiled at her and went on upstairs to his room. There was fresh water in a basin waiting for him, thanks to Laura, and he used it to clean some of the dust off. Later he would take a leisurely bath, but this would do for now.

While he was washing up he thought again about being shot at on the way back from the Millar ranch. Something was definitely up, and he was going to have to keep his eyes wide open.

This was Clint's first dinner with all of the other boarders in the house, and he was formally introduced to them all before he sat down to eat.

Most of them were simply townspeople, merchants or employees who could not yet afford to live anyplace else. There were two people in particular, however, that Clint felt he had some sort of an impact on. One was a man named Frank Williams, who was a clerk in one of the town's stores. He didn't appear to be very happy about Laura Dean's obvious pride as she introduced her new boarder around the table, and he scowled at Clint throughout the meal.

The other person was the young wife of a young man who was a hand on a nearby ranch, and moved off the ranch when he got married. Looking at his wife—and at the way she was looking at him—Clint knew why he had taken her off that ranch and away from those men.

Their names were Bill and Cora Beth Gaines, and Cora was a saucy little blonde with an extremely sensuous face, impudent little breasts that seemed to want to jump off her chest and into a man's hands, and was not shy at all about measuring Clint with her eyes—much to her husband's dismay. Bill Gaines was another man at the table who scowled at Clint the entire time, while his wife Cora Beth was giving the Gunsmith looks of an entirely different kind.

Needless to say, dinner was a strained affair, although the food itself was delicious. In spite of the food, however, Clint made plans right there and then to miss as many meals at the boardinghouse as he could.

After dinner everyone went their own way, and when Clint was on the way out Laura grabbed a hold of his arm.

"Will you be back later?"

"Probably," he said. "But late." He was deliberately being vague, but she didn't seem to notice.

"Well, whenever you get back, just knock on my door."

"That's a good idea, Laura. We have to talk."

"Oh? About what?"

"About our . . . relationship."

"I see. Well, I'll be ready whenever you are."

It wasn't until after he had left that he realized how she might have taken his last remark.

THIRTEEN

"Beer?" Charlie asked when Clint got to the saloon.

"Yeah, a nice cold one."

"How'd you make out at the Millar place?"

"Pat's got all the help he wants; all he's got to do is ask for it."

"He's young," the bartender said, shaking his head.

Clint stopped with the beer halfway to his mouth and asked, "What's that supposed to mean?"

"I mean he's young, and he may not want to ask Mr. Millar for help."

"If he doesn't get any help from the townspeople, he's going to have to ask Millar."

"He's young," Charlie said again. "Young people have a lot of pride."

"Stubborn pride, you mean."

"Exactly."

Clint sipped his beer and then said, "Yeah, well, he's going to have to get over that. A lawman can't afford stubborn pride."

"Your friends are back," Charlie said, indicating

the corner table with the three poker players. "Want to go halves?"

"Why not?" Clint said. "It'll pass the time until Garrett shows up."

By the time Sheriff Pat Garrett did show up Clint was losing by a dollar and bored to tears.

"There's the man I'm waiting for, fellas," he said, picking up his change.

As he was walking away from the table he heard one of them mutter, "There goes our money."

Yeah, he thought, *all fifty-two dollars of it*.

"How'd we do?" Charlie asked.

"You lost a half a dollar," Clint said. He turned to Pat and said, "How'd you do?"

"Let me have a beer, Charlie," Pat said.

"That bad, huh?"

Pat took his beer from Charlie, sipped it and then turned to Clint and said, "It seems that the people in Lancaster are merchants, not gunmen, and I shouldn't expect them to be. I'm the sheriff, and I'm supposed to protect the town. That's what they pay me for."

"Let me have a beer, Charlie," Clint said.

"That's what you expected them to say, isn't it?" Pat asked him.

"Kid—"

"Never mind," the lawman said. "I know, you told me."

"I told you, too," Charlie said, putting Clint's beer down. "What are you going to do now?"

"I don't know," Pat said. "I'll need some deputies, I guess."

He looked at Clint who said, "Don't look at me. We had a deal, remember?"

"You've got me," Charlie said.

"Can you handle a gun?"

"A rifle . . . if what I'm shooting at is holding still."

"Then get me another beer."

Garrett turned to Clint and said, "What lawman lesson does this fall under?"

"Lesson three, how to improvise."

"Well, how do I?"

"You've gone all through town, now it's time for you to go outside of town."

"The ranchers?"

"They've got almost as much invested in this town as the townspeople do. I'm sure you could get some volunteers from—well, take the Millar ranch, for instance."

"There are other ranches for me to go to without bothering Mr. Millar," Pat said.

"Pat, listen—"

"No, Clint, I like the idea. It's a good one. I'm going to get some sleep and then start visiting ranchers tomorrow."

"Where are you sleeping?" Charlie asked.

"In the jailhouse. It's the cheapest place in town." He finished his beer, said good night and left.

"Now what?" Charlie asked Clint.

"He's going to go out and talk to the ranchers tomorrow. Everyone but Millar."

Shaking his head Charlie said, "Millar's got the biggest spread around. He's the only one who'd be able to afford enough men to give the town a chance."

"He'll find that out," Clint said, "and then he'll go to Millar."

"I hope you're right."

Clint hoped he was right too. He didn't relish the

thought of him and Pat Garrett facing off at least a dozen men in the streets of Lancaster while the townspeople watched.

FOURTEEN

Clint had another beer and then walked back to the boardinghouse to turn in for the night. Upstairs, he paused at Laura Dean's door, then shook his head and went into his own room. He'd talk to her in the morning.

As he stepped into his room he heard a sharp intake of breath and drew his gun.

"Don't move," he said to whoever was in the room with him. He reached above the door to turn up the lamp, and the yellow glow showed Cora Beth Gaines waiting for him in his bed.

"Hello, Clint," she said, smiling lewdly. "Can I call you Clint? I mean, after all, we practically live together."

"What are you doing here?"

"I thought I got a message from you this evening, from your eyes," she said. "You certainly got mine, didn't you?"

"Cora Beth, this isn't right—"

"Of course it is," she said, throwing the covers aside. Her breasts were like ripe peaches, firm and full of juice, and her nipples were coppery brown. She slid one hand down her belly until her index finger was buried in her golden thatch and said, "It's the rightest thing in the world."

"Your husband—"

"Is working, won't be back until tomorrow afternoon."

She got up from the bed and approached him, her hand still between her legs.

"I want you, Clint, and you want me," she said, taking her finger away from her crotch now and touching it to his upper lip. "Don't you?"

Her finger was wet with the scent of her and he breathed it in. His tongue flicked out and he tasted the tartness of her juices, and he felt a pounding erection growing inside of his pants. He'd had women try to seduce him before—some successfully, and some not—but none had ever tried this particular ploy.

"You do want me," she said, covering the bulge in his pants with her other hand. "I can tell."

She moved both hands so that she was undoing his pants. She lowered them, then lowered his underwear so she could take his pulsing organ in her hands.

"Oh, yes," she breathed. She went down to her knees and pressed his penis to her face, running it over the smooth skin of her cheeks, her forehead, her chin, then she flicked her tongue out and tasted his fluid as it oozed from his tip.

"Delicious," she said. She opened her mouth wide and took him deep inside and he gasped and grabbed her behind the head. She sucked on him and caressed his sack, reaching behind him to cup his buttocks in her hands. He spread his legs wider as he felt them begin to tremble, and held the back of her head tightly. When he felt that he was going to explode he tried to disengage himself from her, but she wouldn't let him go and when he began to spurt she swallowed every drop and then sucked on him for more.

"Take off the rest of your clothes," she said after releasing him, "and come to bed. We've got a lot of time."

She backed toward the bed and got into it, and he shucked the remainder of his clothes and followed.

He took her in his arms and began to suck on her nipples. She moaned and crushed his face against her breasts. As he suckled her he slid one hand between her legs and found her not only moist but soaked. Remembering the scent on her finger, he kissed his way down her belly, over her golden mound and buried his nose in her wetness. He inhaled her scent deeply, then began to stroke her with his tongue. As he drove his tongue deeply inside of her she moaned aloud and arched her back, and when he began to circle her clit she cried out once before catching herself. Sucking on her, he brought her to a massive orgasm, and by that time his erection was harder and stronger than ever and he was ready again.

He moved up and stabbed into her, causing her breath to catch in her throat.

"Oh, yes," she breathed. "Yes, yes, yes, do it, do it to me, hard, make it hard. . . ."

He began to pound into her powerfully and she came again almost immediately, wrapping her legs and arms around him, showing amazing strength for a small girl. She matched his thrusts, using her muscles to suck on his organ and literally yank his completion from him. As he filled her with his seed she clamped her mouth over his, thrusting her tongue inside, holding the back of his head in her hands and bruising not only his lips, but her own as well.

"Umm," she said against his mouth. "I love kissing, I just love licking and kissing and sucking. Ummm. . . ."

Cora Beth Gaines loved everything that a woman and a man could possibly do together, and during the remainder of the night she did her best to show the Gunsmith just how much there was to love.

FIFTEEN

Early the next morning Cora Beth slipped out of
Clint's room and hurried back to hers without being
seen. At breakfast, however, it became obvious to
Clint that Laura Dean was aware of how he had spent
the night. Her room was, after all, right next to his, and
the walls were rather thin.

She said very little to him during the meal and he
caught her examining both him and Cora Beth at times,
probably because they both had a slight case of swollen
lips. Cora Beth wasn't helping matters either by staring
at him through the whole meal and smiling like that cat
who ate the canary every time Laura looked at her. The
others at the table either didn't take notice or pretended
not to.

After breakfast was over Clint made sure that he was
the first to leave, bidding everyone else a good day. He
didn't want to have to speak to either woman just yet.

He went to the livery and caught up on some gunsmithing work. Consequently he was there when Pat
Garrett came in to get his horse.

"Heading out?" he asked Pat from his wagon.

Pat turned around in surprise, then relaxed when he
saw who it was.

"I thought I'd start with the closest ranches and
work my way out," he said while saddling his horse.

"Aren't there certain ranches you could eliminate right off?"

"Like how?"

"The smaller places that couldn't afford to give you any men, for instance. Maybe you should only go to the large spreads."

Pat shook his head and said, "Most of the spreads around here are pretty small. If they want to save the town, they'll just have to give up some men they can't afford." Mounting up he added, "I won't need them for very long, anyway. Just long enough to turn back the gang."

"And you think that won't take long?"

Shrugging, the big man said, "How long could it take?"

"We'll talk about that when you get back," Clint said. "Good luck."

"Thanks. See you later."

Clint waved and Pat rode out of the livery and was on his way.

The kid was tippytoeing around the possibility of asking Ken Millar for help, Clint noticed. It was that young, stubborn pride at work. When he got back they were going to have to work at overcoming that. He was going to need the men that Millar could give him, and he was going to need them for a lot longer than he thought. The sooner Clint got Pat Garrett to realize that, the better off they would all be.

Clint went back inside his wagon and got back to work, but after about a half an hour he became aware that someone else was in the livery. It could have been the liveryman or the blacksmith, who worked in the back, but after two shooting incidents he wasn't about to take anything for granted.

He moved to the rear door of his wagon, his hand hovering near his gun, and peered out. He was surprised to find Laura Dean inching her way into the livery, obviously looking around for someone.

"Laura," he said, and she started and jumped at the sound of his voice.

"Oh, Clint," she said when she saw him. "You scared me."

"Sneaking around like that is a good way to get yourself killed," he told her, dropping to the ground.

"I wasn't sneaking," she said, defensively. "I was just . . . looking . . ."

"For what?"

"For you."

"Why?"

"To talk. Remember yesterday you said you wanted to talk about our relationship?"

"I didn't think we had one anymore . . . after last night."

"What about last night?"

"Come on, Laura. We said right at the outset that there would be no games between us."

"That's what I thought too."

"Laura, about last night—"

"Is that why you did it? Because you wanted me to hear you and break off—"

"I didn't plan that," he hastened to tell her. "When I got to my room, Cora Beth was in my bed."

"Why didn't you stop at my room?" she asked. "Is it because she's younger—"

"That's got nothing to do with anything," he said, cutting her off. "Laura, I never said we'd have a lasting relationship."

"I know that . . . now," she said. "But Cora Beth—"

"You don't like her," Clint said.

"She's a tease, and she does it right under her husband's nose. The poor boy doesn't know what to do. He didn't know what he was getting himself into when he married her."

"Look, if you want me to move out, I will."

"I didn't say that," she said. "I just want to—to know how you feel."

"I like you a lot, Laura," he said, "and I enjoy being with you. Cora Beth—that was a one-time thing. She was there, and she was naked and I am, after all, human."

"And male," Laura added, "and she seems to have a profound effect on all males."

"You can't deny that she's lovely."

"No, regretfully, I can't."

"I don't have any intention of repeating my, uh, experience with Cora Beth . . . but I can't make any promises about her or any other woman."

Laura took a moment to think about it, then said, "I don't expect you to make any promises, Clint. You just tell me when you want me, and I'll be ready. I almost feel ashamed saying that, but I don't really. I know you won't be in town for long, and I know there won't be another man after you leave—not for a while, anyway."

"What about Frank Williams?"

"Frank has let it be known on several occasions that he'd like to share my bed, but he never has and he never will." They stared at each other through an awkward silence, and then she said, "Well, I've had my say, and you have work to do."

"Laura—"

"Let's not say any more, Clint. I'm going to go back to the house and clean it from top to bottom, and try and keep from strangling Cora Beth. I wish poor Bill Gaines would get smart and leave her.''

"He loves her,'' Clint said.

"Yes, he does,'' she agreed, ''and that's his biggest problem.'' She started for the door, then turned and said, ''Sometimes I think that love is everyone's biggest problem.''

"Love is a problem that comes with living,'' Clint said to her. ''But *living*—that's everyone's *biggest* problem.''

SIXTEEN

When Clint finished his day's work and had returned the repaired weapons to their owners—and been paid—he went over to the saloon for a cold beer and some conversation with Charlie Anderson.

"Has Pat gotten back yet?" Charlie asked him.

"No," Clint said, "and I guess I would have known if he had. I've been working in the livery all day."

"I wonder what kind of luck he's having."

"He's going to have to make up his mind right quick about asking some of the Millar ranch boys to stand with him. The Chambers gang should be here soon."

"How long you figure?"

"Couple of days, at the outside."

Charlie pursed his lips and whistled soundlessly. "And they're supposed to have at least a dozen men, right?"

"At least."

"Why would anyone want to be a lawman?"

"I've wondered that a few times myself during my life, Charlie," the Gunsmith said.

"Looks like our friends have found themselves a new pigeon," the bartender said, changing the subject.

Clint turned and saw that his poker buddies had indeed found another fourth to play with.

69

"You backing him?"

Charlie shook his head and said, "I know a born loser when I see one."

Clint looked back at the man, who seemed dressed well enough in trail clothes that were dusty, but not particularly worn.

"He doesn't look like such a loser to me."

"Watch."

Clint finished his beer and had another, watching the game the whole time, and the stranger was losing steadily. He wasn't being cheated, but when three other players are all playing against you, it can come out almost the same way.

"That ain't possible," the stranger finally shouted, throwing down his hand.

"Mister, you just plumb got bad luck at cards," Red said, reaching for his pot.

"I ain't never been this unlucky," the stranger said. "You fellas have been cheating me."

"Mister, that's a harsh word," Andy said.

"I don't like being cheated," the man said, and stood up quickly. His chair would have fallen over if he hadn't been sitting against the wall. Instead, he found himself with his legs and hips pinned between the chair and the table.

"Take it easy—" Red started to say, but the man reached under the table and overturned it, bellowing angrily. Red went over backwards, while the other two players scrambled out of the way.

Clint saw what was coming next very clearly. He stepped away from the bar with his beer still in his right hand and shouted, "Hold it, mister."

Everybody froze and looked over at the Gunsmith. The stranger saw a tall, slim man standing very relaxed, with a beer in his gun hand.

"Don't pull that gun out," Clint said.

"Why not? You gonna stop me from giving these card cheats what they deserve?"

"They're not card cheats, mister. You're just a mighty bad poker player. You face that truth, and you'll stay alive."

"Meaning what?"

"Meaning if you go for that gun, I'm going to have to drop you where you stand."

"You the law in this town?"

"I'm as close as you'll get, right now."

"You think you can outdraw me while holding that beer in your hand?" the man asked.

"That's for you to find out, friend . . . any time you're ready."

The room was filled with the sound of chairs scraping the floor as the rest of the customers vacated their chairs and tables to find refuge from flying lead.

The stranger stared at Clint, noticing that his eyes were steady, as was the hand holding the beer, and suddenly decided that ten dollars in change was not enough to die for.

"Are you gonna lock me up?"

"I don't have the authority to lock you up," Clint said.

"But you have the authority to kill me."

"Again, my friend, that's entirely up to you."

The stranger held both of his hands up in front of his chest, palms out, and said, "Listen, all I want to do now is walk out of here, mount up and ride."

"Then do it."

The man sidled towards the batwing doors, keeping his eyes on Clint all the way. When he reached the doors he turned and rushed through them, and a few seconds later the sound of hoofbeats broke the silence as the stranger rode out of town.

Clint turned to Charlie Anderson and set his beer down on the bar. "I think that one's a little warm now, Charlie," he said. "Could you get me a cold one?"

"Sure, Clint, sure," Charlie said, staring at the Gunsmith in awe.

When he brought back the beer he said, "Jesus, Clint, but you scared the shit out of *me;* I can imagine how that poor stranger felt."

"That poor stranger was very close to killing three men over some change," Clint said.

"And even closer to getting killed himself, right? You would have killed him if he had drawn, wouldn't you?"

Clint stared at Charlie, but before he could answer Red came over while the other two players were righting the table and picking up the scattered money and cards.

"I'd, uh, just like to thank you, Clint," he stammered. "I think maybe you saved our lives just now."

"You've got to watch who you play poker with in the future, Red," Clint told him. "There are a lot of sore losers in the world."

"I know," Red said. "Yeah, I know that. Uh, the boys, they, uh, just wanted me to tell you that, uh—"

"What, Red?"

"Uh, you can forget about that money of ours you won. If you don't, uh, want to play anymore you don't—uh, don't feel that you have to give us a chance to get it back. Okay?"

The look on Red's face was so hopeful that Clint simply said, "Okay, Red, if that's the way you boys want it."

Red nodded and went back to his table.

"What do you make of that?" Clint asked Charlie.

Charlie shrugged and said, "I guess you scared the shit out of them too."

SEVENTEEN

Clint chose to bypass Laura's door again that night and go right to his room. When he got inside and turned up the lamp he was pleased to find his bed empty. He didn't feel like dealing with Cora Beth Gaines tonight. He was sure that her husband was not working tonight, and that was why she hadn't come.

He undressed and sat on his bed, thinking about what he was doing in Lancaster. He had made a few dollars fixing guns—not much, but certainly enough to move on to the next town. If it weren't for Pat Garrett, that was just what he would be doing come morning, but he owed young Pat his life, and that debt was keeping him here—but to do what? To meet his own death when he and Garrett were forced to face the Chambers gang alone?

No, part of his debt was to show Pat Garrett how to be a lawman, and a lawman asked for help when he needed it. Pat had to ask Ken Millar for help, whether he wanted to or not, and Clint was going to have to make him realize that.

He stood up, turned down the lamp and then got into bed without pulling the covers over him.

He didn't know how long he'd been asleep when something woke him up. His gun was hanging on the bedpost, as always, within fast and easy reach, but for now he just relaxed, waited and listened.

Women had come to him before in the darkness. It's always the smell that gives them away, then the rustle of their clothing against their flesh when they undress.

He felt someone grab the covers at the base of the bed, and then she got in with him, drawing the covers over them. It wasn't Laura, because Laura was bigger, her breasts were larger. The pair of breasts that were pressed against his back were small and firm. The girl reached between his legs from behind and began to stroke him, and then her hot mouth descended on his neck and shoulders.

It had to be Cora Beth.

He turned around to face her and she crept in against him, kissing his chest and reaching down to hold onto his erection. It had gone past the point where he could tell her to leave. His penis was much too involved for that, right now.

"You have to be quiet," he told her, and she pressed her mouth against his and said, "Mmm-hmm."

He kissed her, explored the inside of her mouth with his tongue, then began to nibble and kiss her breasts and nipples until she was squirming around underneath him, and he was inside of her and in order to keep quiet she was biting his shoulders, making it hard for him to keep quiet.

He reached underneath her to cup her small buttocks in his palms and, using his arms, drew her in to him every time *he* drove into her. Finally she gasped aloud, and she was bucking beneath him while her body was racked with the spasms of her pleasure.

"Cora Beth—" he said, but before he could go on she said into his ear, "I'm not Cora Beth."

"What?" he said, puzzled. She sure felt like Cora Beth, although now that he thought about it, her responses were a bit different than the night before. She seemed a bit less experienced, but more eager.

"Then who are you?" he asked, a question to which the only answer he received was a giggle.

He got up, crossed to the lamp and turned it up. When he turned around he was facing neither Laura Dean nor Cora Beth Gaines.

Lying in his bed, naked and looking very satisfied with herself—and with him, no doubt—was Donna Millar, Ken Millar's seventeen-year-old niece.

EIGHTEEN

"I'm eighteen, actually," she informed him.

"That's not the point, Donna," he said, sitting at the foot of the bed. "Where does your uncle think you are this late at night?"

"Probably with Pat," she said, shrugging her shoulders prettily. "I think he always wished I'd marry Pat, but we're not interested in each other." Leaning forward and wetting her lips she said, "On the other hand, I'm very interested in you—and I think you're interested in me too. Who did you think I was? Who's Cora Beth?"

"Never mind who I thought you were," he said. "Now that I know who you are it's time for you to get out of here."

"And go where?" she asked. "Are you going to make me ride all the way back to the Bar M alone late at night?"

"No," he conceded. "I can't very well do that."

"Then I'll just stay here until morning," she said, burrowing under his covers.

"No, you can't stay here."

"Where can I go?"

He could have taken her over to the hotel and gotten her a room, but then word would have gotten back to Millar that she had been seen with him.

"You wanted me to keep quiet," she reminded him. "If you try and make me leave, I'm going to start yelling."

"Don't be childish."

"Sometimes being childish is a good way to get what you want," she told him wisely. "Like now."

He stared at her, realizing that she had him—for now—where she wanted him, and said, "All right, you can stay tonight, but first thing in the morning you get back to the ranch."

"I have to buy a new dress, first. We're having a party at the ranch, and I came to invite you. Uncle said I should."

"All right, you invited me, now go to sleep."

"Come to bed," she said.

"No, you sleep in the bed, I'll sleep in that chair," he said, indicating the straight-backed wooden chair by the window.

"Now who's being childish?" she demanded. "You'll hurt your neck and your back sleeping in that chair. It's not as if we didn't already do anything. You'd think I was a virgin or something. Now stop being silly and come to bed," she scolded him, throwing back the covers. In the glow of the lamp he saw that her body was lovely, if not yet fully developed. Her breasts were firm and round and would probably fill out and get a little larger. Her belly was rounded slightly, as if she still had a bit of baby fat, but that would vanish in a year or so.

"You're a lovely girl, Donna," he said, "and you're going to be a very beautiful woman."

"Do you really think so?" she asked, her face betraying the pleasure she gained from the remark.

"Yes, I do."

"Come to bed, then, Clint."

"Move over and behave, and I'll come to bed," he said, finally.

"Good!" she exclaimed, moving over to make room for him.

He turned down the lamp and then walked to the bed and got in beside her. Immediately her warm hip was thrust against him, and her hand fluttered onto him beneath the covers.

"Donna, I said behave," he reminded her, catching hold of her hand.

"If you don't make love to me I'll start yelling," she threatened.

"You wouldn't."

"Oh, yes, I would. I'm being childish, remember?"

"You're not giving me much of a choice," he complained.

"Oh, Clint, didn't you enjoy what we just did?" she asked.

He hesitated a moment, then said, "Yes, I did enjoy it."

"Then just relax and enjoy it again. It's not going to hurt anyone, and there are things I want to do with you that I've never dared try with anyone else."

"Like what?"

She freed her hand from his and said, "Like this."

Burrowing underneath the covers with her head she came to rest with her nose nestled between his legs. He felt her tongue flick out tentatively and lick the head of his penis, and then she became bolder. Holding his penis with both hands she began to suck eagerly on the tip, and then slid more and more of it into her mouth until she was sucking on most of it, with one hand holding the base, and the other holding his sack.

"Jesus," he muttered, moving his hips in time with the bobbing motion of her head.

"I want you to shoot in my mouth," she said from beneath the covers.

"Just keep on doing what you're doing," he told her, "and you'll get what you want."

"Good," she said, and her eager, hot mouth recaptured his penis and began to suck furiously again.

Well, he thought, *at least with her head under the covers like that no one will be able to hear her.*

NINETEEN

In the morning he woke up with her nose nuzzling his flaccid penis.

"Jesus, what are you trying to do, girl, kill me?"

She giggled and pressed her face flat against his crotch. He reached beneath the covers, put his hands under her arms and drew her up until she was lying flat on top of him with her little breasts crushed against his chest.

"Oh," she said, rubbing her breasts against him. "I love the way the hair on your chest tickles my nipples."

"Never mind," he said, slapping her on the behind. "It's time for you to get out of here."

"Oh, pooh."

"The time for childishness is now past, Donna. You've got to leave before the rest of the house wakes up."

"Like Cora Beth?"

He slapped her behind again, a resounding slap that was muffled by the covers.

"Ouch," she squealed.

"That's what you need," he told her. "A good spanking."

"I'd rather have a good stuffing," she said, wiggling her hips and giving him a lewd look. She was a lot like Cora Beth, this young girl, or the way Cora Beth probably was six or seven years ago. He hoped Donna would grow out of it, as Cora Beth had obviously not.

He watched her dress and had to admit that it was as pretty a sight as a man would ever want to see. Her legs had developed beyond the rest of her body, and the muscles rippled beneath the skin as she slipped into her jeans. When she was dressed she tied her cornsilk hair with a pink ribbon.

"How did you get in here, anyway?" he asked her when she was ready to go.

"A back window was open and I slipped in after everyone was asleep."

"Well, see if you can slip out the same way. I don't want the whole house to wake up in an uproar."

"I'll be careful," she promised. She approached the bed and leaned over to be kissed, only when he went to kiss her she opened her mouth and sucked his tongue in until he thought it would tear from the roots.

"Donna, don't do this again," he warned her.

"Then you think of a way for us to be together," she said. "I'll leave it up to you."

"Fine."

She started for the door, then turned and said, "Oh, yes, the party. It's to be tomorrow night, and it's for my eighteenth birthday—which is today," she added, grinning at him. "Guess what I got myself for a present?"

"Get out of here, you," he said, and when she was gone he found himself laughing and shaking his head.

Laura Dean, Cora Beth Gaines and now Donna Millar. Often it was nice—and it really didn't happen all that often—to have three women eager for your attentions, but juggling these three was potentially a dangerous situation. Donna was very young, and the niece of the most powerful rancher in the area, who seemed to want to match her with young Pat Garrett. Cora Beth was also young, though six or seven years older than Donna, but she was already married, which made her the most dangerous of the three, especially since she also lived in the boardinghouse with her husband.

And then there was Laura Dean, the oldest, but definitely not giving anything away to the two younger women in the way of beauty and eagerness, only she was making too much out of a brief relationship even though she had apparently agreed to take it as it came.

Three lovely, delightful and dangerous women—a totally different sort of gang than the one he and Pat were waiting for.

Thinking of the Chambers gang—and it was an odd segue, to say the least—he decided to get up and get out, avoiding breakfast with the rest of the household. There was a café near the saloon where he'd had a few meals, and he'd go there for a leisurely breakfast before seeking out Pat Garrett and finding out what progress he had made during his visit to the area ranchers.

Clint was lingering over his second pot of strong, black coffee when Pat Garrett saved him the trouble of looking for him by walking right in and sitting down with him. It was early and Clint was the only customer in the place.

"What are you doing up so early?" he asked Pat. "You must have gotten back pretty late last night."

"Very late."

The waitress brought over another cup and Pat helped himself to some coffee.

"The way you're drinking that you look as if you wish it were something stronger."

"I'm a little discouraged, Clint," Pat confessed. "I

can't understand these people; the townspeople, the ranchers—they all seem to have the same attitude."

"You do it," Clint said, "or let someone else do it."

"I know you've probably dealt with this kind of thing before—"

"Over and over. That badge makes you a target, Pat, in more ways than one.

"I'm starting to realize that."

"You want something to eat?"

"I'm not hungry."

"Okay, here's another lawman lesson. Listen up! You've got to eat, you've got to keep your strength up, as well as your chin. In a way these people are right."

"What?"

"Sure, you're getting paid to take care of the likes of the Chambers gang, they aren't. You're the sheriff, not them."

"So what do I do now?"

"What do *we* do now?"

"Clint, I'm not going to ask you to stand by me if it's only going to be the two of us facing that gang," Pat told him.

"But you'll stand alone if you have to."

"What else can I do?"

"I'm not going to let you stand alone, Pat, but you haven't exhausted all of your possibilities yet. Without even asking you, I know you didn't go to the Millar ranch to ask for help. Am I right?"

Pat set his chin and said, "Yes, you're right, but—"

"But you've got your reasons."

"Yes."

"Crap! That's a lot of crap, Pat. Your first responsibility as sheriff of Lancaster is to this town, and not to your own personal pride."

"It's not—"

"It's stubborn pride, but that comes from youth. I'll tell you something, Pat, and you keep this in mind if you want to go on being a lawman." He hesitated to make sure he had Garrett's full attention, then explained. "Lawmen are supposed to be an ageless breed, untouched by the problems of either youth or age. They don't give in to stubborn pride, or aching muscles and brittle bones."

Sheriff Pat Garrett poured himself some more coffee and kept a stoic expression on his face.

Clint leaned across the table and poked him in his chest with considerable force. "You've got to decide if you're really serious about making the law your life, Pat."

"And if I don't go to Mr. Millar it means I'm not?"

"Exactly."

"That's too cut and dried for me," Pat said. "There's got to be leeway—"

"Believe me when I tell you that I spent a lot of years looking, and there isn't any. It's one way or the other."

When the waitress came Clint ordered another pot of coffee and the same breakfast that he'd had for the young lawman.

When she left, Clint asked, "Are you going to go to him?"

"I haven't decided."

"Well, you better decide pretty damn quick," the Gunsmith said. "How much longer do you think we've got before the Chambers gang gets here? No, don't guess, I'll tell you. One, maybe two days. No more." Clint leaned forward and said, "We've got to know how many men we can depend on—today, Pat—so we can make our plans to defend this town."

Pat looked annoyed and drank some more coffee.

"Look, I understand there's a party at the ranch tonight. If you approach him then, we can make our plans overnight and put them into effect in the morning."

"What kind of plans?"

"We need four men, one each at points north, south, east and west of town."

"Lookouts?"

"Right. At first sight of the gang a man will ride back here and tell us; this way we'll be ready for them, whether there's two of us, or twenty."

The waitress brought Pat's breakfast and he stared at it morosely.

"Oh, go on and eat it. It's on me."

"I'll pay for it," Pat said, picking up his fork. "I don't intend to be one of those lawmen who takes meals for nothing."

"Admirable," Clint said. "I only hope you don't feel the same way about accepting help—especially from your friends."

TWENTY

The Chambers gang was about two days ride from Lancaster when Jeff Wall and Billy Field met up with them.

"This wasn't exactly what I had in mind," Wall told Field as the two of them were disarmed and tied up.

"Well, tell them what we want, Jeff," Field said, looking frightened. "Explain it to them."

"I will, as soon as I get a chance," Wall assured him.

"Shut up," one of the men holding them said. "You'll get your chance to talk."

"That's all I ask," Wall said.

"Sit," he was told, and both he and Field were pushed down to the ground.

After a couple of hours they were approached by four men who all resembled each other in one way or another.

"Okay," one of them told the man who was guarding the two trussed-up men. He nodded and walked off.

The oldest looking of the four turned to Wall and Field and said, "I'm told you been looking for us."

"We have if you're the Chambers brothers."

"We are," the man said. "I'm Willy Chambers. These are my brothers."

"I'm Jeff Wall, and this is Billy Field. We've come to, uh, join up with you."

"Why should you want to do that?" Willy asked. "And why should we let you?"

"If you could untie us and let us have a cup of coffee and something to eat—"

"We don't share our food with strangers, friend," Willy said. "It's only for the gang."

"Well, once we join—"

"You still ain't told us why we should let you," Matt said.

"Shut up, Matt," Willy said. "Let the man talk." To Wall he said, "Go ahead, talk."

Wall talked about Lancaster, which was a subject of great interest to Willy Chambers. He talked about Pat Garrett and about Clint Adams.

"That's the one they call the Gunsmith, isn't it?" Willy asked.

"That's right."

"And you tried to ambush him?"

"Twice," Billy Field spoke up. "But it wasn't my fault that we missed."

"Shut up," Wall said, because he thought it would appeal to Willy Chambers. "We tried to get him once before we knew who he was, and once after."

"Why?"

"The first time for money, what we could get from him, and the second time—well, because of who he is."

Willy Chambers took a few steps forward so that he was standing directly above Wall and said, "It's because of who he is that he deserves better than to be ambushed by a couple of cowards."

"Hey—"

Willy turned around and walked away, past his brothers.

"Willy, what do you want to do with them?" Seth called out.

Willy turned and said, "My first instinct is to kill them, but they're not worth the lead it would take. Put another guard on them until I make up my mind."

"Where are you going now?"

Willy turned and walked away, saying over his shoulder, "To talk to Stud."

"The Gunsmith?" Stud asked, his eyes shining.

"That's what I'm told, but I'm not sure I can trust the information. That's why I want you to ride ahead and make sure."

"The Gunsmith," Stud said again, savoring the name.

"Damn it, Stud, stop salivating. Don't take him on until we get there."

"It'll be hard to resist," Stud said, "but I'll give it a shot."

"That's what I don't want you to give it," Willy said. "I just want to know what we're dealing with. If Adams is there, it could change our whole approach."

"He would make a difference," Stud agreed, "if any one man could."

Willy leaned back and asked, "How good is he, Stud?"

"Well, I've never actually seen him, but I saw Hickok, and the Gunsmith's supposed to be just about as good."

"And how good are you, Stud?"

"I'm the best, Willy," Stud said. "But don't worry, we won't tell anybody."

Willy shifted uncomfortably.

"You can make your brothers and the rest of these empty heads think what you want, Willy. I don't care." Stud stood up and dumped the remains of his coffee into the fire, causing it to flare. "Just don't start believing it yourself. See you in Lancaster."

TWENTY-ONE

When the stranger rode into town, nobody noticed him. He was unremarkable in appearance, less than average height and dressed no better or worse than most cowhands. His horse was a tired bay mare who had seen better days, but that didn't matter to him. He was not a man who named a horse that he rode, because a horse was just a way of getting from one place to another without walking. Did you name a train when you rode one?

He put the mare up in the livery and asked directions to the nearest hotel. Checking into the hotel he signed his real name, which meant nothing in particular to the clerk: John Stud.

Up in his room, overlooking the street, Stud thought back to a time when he was in Oklahoma and had seen Wild Bill Hickok. By that time, as a young man, he had already killed five men, but was still awed by Hickok's speed. To this day he was convinced that he was a more accurate shot than Hickok ever was, but he was not as sure as he let on that he could have outdrawn the man—and now he'd never know.

The only way he could come close to knowing was to take on the Gunsmith.

Leaving his room he walked until he came to a saloon, then went in and ordered a beer.

"Just get into town, did you?" the bartender asked.

"That's right."

"Passing through?"

Stud sipped his beer, then looked at the bartender with cold, dead eyes. "Friendly type aren't you?"

"Sure am," the bartender answered. "Catch more flies with honey than you do—"

"Well, I'm not," the man went on, ignoring the bartender's inane remarks. "I just came in here for a beer, not for conversation. When I want to talk to you, I'll let you know."

The bartender seemed stung for a moment, then shrugged and said, "Have it your way, friend."

"I'm not your friend."

The bartender shrugged again and walked down to the other end of the bar, which suited John Stud just fine.

Stud disliked people intensely. Even riding with the Chambers gang caused him more displeasure than anything else, but he wouldn't be with them for long. After this Lancaster thing—burning it and looting it—he'd take his share and head on by himself. Willy Chambers was getting on his nerves more and more with his posturing and preening. Nothing would have suited him more than to outdraw the fool in front of his brothers and everyone else and shoot him dead, but there was no profit in it.

Of course, what happened after he got his share was entirely up to Chambers.

He noticed a very small stakes poker game going on in a corner of the room and thought that it might be a good way to pass the time. He wasn't much of a card player, so the size of the game didn't matter much to him.

He walked over to the table. "Mind if I sit in?"

"Sure, stranger, help yourself," one of the men said. "My name's Red."

Stud looked at him and said, "Let's play cards."

Red stared at the man a moment, then shrugged and figured if the man didn't want to trade names, that was his business.

"Dealer's choice, friend. Two bits minimum."

Stud allowed the man to call him "friend" simply to avoid further conversation. He merely nodded and picked up his cards as they were dealt to him.

He played for a half hour, losing steadily, and then signaled the bartender to bring him another beer.

Charlie Anderson brought the beer over and removed the empty mug, tried to catch Red's eye without success. He was amazed that Red and the others hadn't learned their lesson from the incident of the previous evening. This man they were playing with now was definitely trouble, although he hardly looked it—until you looked into his eyes.

He went back to the bar and kept an eye on the game, hoping that Clint would come walking in, or at least Pat Garrett, although he had his doubts about whether the young lawman could handle the stranger, except in a fist fight. Pat was a giant of a man, while the stranger was less than average size, very slim and had very small hands.

Still, as small as he was, Charlie was sure that he was a king-sized package of trouble.

He watched the game, hoping desperately that the man would start winning.

TWENTY-TWO

Clint was in his room at the boardinghouse getting dressed for the party at the Millar ranch while John Stud was playing low-stakes poker.

"How'd you find out about the party?" Pat had asked him earlier.

"From Donna Millar," Clint answered. "I guess she was coming to town to do some shopping and her uncle asked her to invite me."

"Why? I mean, no offense, but you've never met either of them, have you?"

Clint was stopped by that question. Did he want Pat to know that he'd ridden out to the Millar place? Eventually, yes, but not right now. Not while Pat was still making up his mind whether or not to ask his old employer for help.

"I guess maybe Mayor Gault told him I was here," he said, finally. "I do have something of a reputation, you know."

"I know, although I get the feeling you don't like the idea."

"Let's just say that sometimes—a lot of times—it gets in the way of my being left alone."

He left his room now and walked downstairs. Pat and he were supposed to meet at the livery and ride out together. On the way out he ran into Cora Beth.

"My, what are you all duded up for?" she asked, posing coyly.

"A party."

"Can you bring a guest?"

"I'm already someone else's guest, Cora Beth, so I don't think it would be proper."

"Oh, who cares about what's proper?"

"You don't, obviously," he said.

"What's that mean?"

"It means that what happened between us the other night should not happen again."

"It shouldn't?"

"No. I'm not looking for any trouble with your husband."

"Oh, Clint, Bill couldn't give you any trouble that you couldn't handle, and you know it."

"I'd rather not have to handle it, Cora Beth. You're just going to have to find someone else to entertain you when your husband is away."

"I need a real man, Clint," she said, "and the only one around right now is you."

"Give your husband a chance, Cora Beth, and maybe he'll prove himself to you."

"He's had his chance," she said, "and you should know that I don't give up easy."

"That's a shame, because you're only going to be disappointed."

"We'll see about that," she said, firmly, and flounced off.

When Clint turned to head for the door he found himself facing Laura Dean.

"You heard?"

"I didn't mean to."

"That's all right. I'm glad you did."

"I'm glad I did too," she said. "Have a good time at the party."

"If I could bring a guest, Laura, it would be you."

He left, pleased at the way things had turned out with Laura. Cora Beth, however, was another matter entirely. Bill Gaines had not said much to Clint since their meeting, but he had no doubt that if the young man found out about him and Cora Beth, he'd come after the Gunsmith with his youthful pride stung, and not think about the consequences first.

Clint hoped to avoid that, for the boy's sake as well as his own.

He met Pat at the livery, saddling his horse, a good-looking pinto. While saddling Duke he said, "How about stopping at the saloon for a quick drink before heading for the ranch?"

"Sounds fine to me," Pat said.

They mounted up headed for the saloon.

"I saw Donna earlier," Pat said.

"Did you?"

"She was picking up a new dress she ordered, and then she went back to the ranch."

"She's a pretty little thing, isn't she?" Clint asked.

"I guess, but I'm a big man, Clint, and I prefer a big woman. I think Mr. Millar always hoped that I'd take to Donna, and she to me, but it just never worked out."

"Well, that's unfortunate for him, but neither of you can live your lives for him."

"That's right."

They pulled up in front of the saloon and went inside. The look of absolute relief on Charlie Anderson's face when they walked through the door did not escape the Gunsmith's attention.

"What's the matter with you, Charlie?" he asked as

they approached the bar. "You look like the savior just walked in."

"Maybe he did," Charlie said. "Red and the others have gotten themselves another player, Clint, and this one looks like trouble."

"Why?" Clint asked. He and Pat looked over at the poker table, where all four players seemed engrossed in the game. The fourth player was sitting with his back to the wall, examining his cards, and didn't look particularly like trouble—but then, the man the night before hadn't much looked like trouble, either.

"I meant to ask about last night," Pat said.

"It wasn't anything," Clint said. "Just what you would have done if you were here."

"From what I hear I might have done it a bit differently, though," Pat said. He turned to Charlie and said, "How about a couple of beers?"

"Sure," Charlie said, keeping his eyes on the table in the corner.

"Charlie," Clint said when he brought the beers, "what makes you think this guy is trouble."

"His eyes," the bartender answered immediately. "His eyes gave me a chill like I ain't never had before, Clint. I know he don't look like much, but when you look at his eyes you get a whole different idea about him."

Clint turned and looked at the man again, but there was nothing familiar about him.

"You want us to stick around?" he asked Charlie.

"Well, if he was still losing I'd say yes, but for the past half hour he's been cleaning up."

"Really? He must be a whole ten dollars ahead by now," Clint said. "I'll tell you what." Clint turned to Pat. "You go on to the party and I'll stay here for a while."

"No, if one of us is going to stay—" Pat started to protest, but Clint didn't allow him to go any further.

"You have to go out there, remember?" he said. "You have something to talk to Mr. Millar about."

"Yeah, but if there's gonna be trouble—"

"There's not going to be any trouble, Pat," Clint assured him. "Just go on out to the party; I'll be along in a while."

Pat looked into his beer and said, "All right, I'll go." He finished his beer and put the empty mug down on the bar. Looking over at the poker table again he said, "Let me know what happens."

"Nothing is going to happen, believe me. Just go and do what you have to do."

"I'm going."

"Have a good time, while you're there. Tomorrow, one way or another, it's going to be all business."

"Yeah," Pat said. "I'll see you in a while."

When the big man left the saloon Clint told Charlie to get him another beer, and then he settled down to watch the proceedings at the poker table.

"We're being watched," Stud said. He had noticed the two men enter the saloon, talk to the bartender, and then become very interested in what was going on at the table. He had seen all of that without seeming to.

Red turned his head to see what the stranger meant, then said, "Hell, that's just Clint Adams."

"And the big man who was with him?"

"That must have been the new sheriff, Pat Garrett."

"Kind of young for that job, isn't he?"

Red looked at the stranger curiously, wondering why all of a sudden he didn't mind talking. "I guess. It's your deal, stranger."

"Yeah," Stud said, picking up the cards. "Why does that name sound familiar, Clint Adams?"

"Maybe 'cause they call him the Gunsmith," Andy suggested.

"That's right," Stud said. "I remember that." Dealing the cards he said, "So that's the Gunsmith, huh?" Stud's heart was racing at that moment, and it had nothing to do with the fact that he'd dealt himself a pat hand.

He would have liked nothing better than to stand up at that moment and call Clint Adams out, outdraw and kill him in front of witnesses. That would establish John Stud as the best man, better than the Gunsmith, better than Hickok, better than anyone.

"Hey," Red called across the table.

"Yeah?"

"It's your play."

Stud stared at the man for a few seconds, then said, "You're so right."

TWENTY-THREE

After an hour of watching the game, nothing untoward had happened and Clint was just finishing up what was to be his last beer.

"I'm going to get going, Charlie," he said to the bartender. "Everything looks under control here."

"I guess," Charlie said, though he looked somewhat dubious.

"You say he just arrived in town today?"

"That's right, that's what he said."

"All right. Before I leave town I'll check the hotel and see what his name is."

Charlie nodded and then looked over at the table again. "I just don't want my place busted up."

"Charlie, everything's all right," Clint said. "Relax."

"Sure. Look, go and have a good time. I'm sorry I made you waste an hour."

"No problem."

Clint started to dig into his pocket for money when Charlie said, "Forget it. I kept you here, I'll foot the bill."

"You sure?"

"Go."

"Thanks, Charlie. See you—probably tomorrow."

"Yeah," Charlie muttered as Clint left, "if my place is still here tomorrow."

John Stud noticed Clint Adams leaving, and his chance was gone—for now. Actually, he had let the opportunity pass. There was more profit in waiting for the Chambers brothers to arrive than in taking him now.

"Well, well," he said, playing his cards out to reveal the winning hand, "it looks like I'm on some kind of winning streak." *The biggest kind.*

Clint walked Duke over to the hotel and went inside to talk to the clerk.

"I'd like to see your register for today."

"Why?"

"Sheriff Garrett asked me to have a look."

"Why ain't he lookin' himself?" the clerk asked.

Clint leaned on the counter and told the rat-faced man, "Because he asked me to do him a favor. You wouldn't want to keep me from doing him a favor, would you?"

The clerk backed away from the Gunsmith's stare and the register magically presented itself for his examination.

He turned the pages until he reached the day's date and saw that there had only been one entry. It had to be the stranger who was playing cards in the saloon, and this surprised Clint to some degree.

He would have expected John Stud to be a much bigger man.

"Thanks," he said to the clerk, closing the book and pushing it across the desk.

He went out and stood with his hand on Duke's

neck, wondering now if it would be wise to leave town and go to the Millar place. Why not? Just because the stranger turned out to be a gunman with a reputation didn't change the fact that he was over in the saloon playing poker.

Still, this was just one more coincidence that Clint Adams didn't believe in. *I'm shot at twice, the Chambers gang is coming to town, and now John Stud shows up.*

This was all building up to something, and now he knew that he'd better get out to the Millar ranch and make sure that Pat Garrett asked Millar for help.

They were going to need all the help they could get.

TWENTY-FOUR

The party was largely inside the house, with some of it spilling out into the back. When Clint arrived he gave Duke over to a suitably impressed ranch hand and went on inside.

Pat Garrett was an easy man to pick, as he towered over most of the other guests. There wasn't a man there who was anywhere near his size. The young lawman was standing across the room, talking to Donna Millar.

"Is everything all right?" Pat said as Clint came up on them.

"Everything's fine, Pat," Clint assured him, patting him on the back. "No problems. Hello, Miss Millar."

"Oh, call me Donna, please."

"All right, Donna."

"Can I get you a drink?" she asked. "Whiskey, or a beer?"

"A beer would be fine . . . and by the way, happy birthday."

"Thank you very much," she said. "I'll get you that beer."

"Fine."

When she left Pat said, "Tell me what happened."

"I checked with the hotel to see who had checked in today. Does the name John Stud mean anything to you?"

"Stud, John Stud," Pat repeated. "There's something familiar about it—"

"There should be. Stud is a top gunman, very well-known in some parts of the country. He's not widely known yet, but that would appear to be a matter of time."

"And you're telling me that the man playing cards in the saloon is John Stud?"

"Right."

Pat put his beer down and said, "I've got to get back to town, then."

"Why?"

"There's a major gunman in my town," Pat said. "I shouldn't be at a party."

"Have you talked to Mr. Millar yet about getting some help?"

"Uh, no, I haven't been able to corner him."

Clint looked across the room and said, "Well, there he is, all cornered for you. Do you want me to come with you?"

"No," Pat said. "I can do this on my own, Clint."

"Yes, I noticed."

"All right, I'll go and talk to him and then I'm getting back to town."

"I'll come with you. We've got plans to make, remember?"

"Right."

Clint watched Pat walk across the room, engage Millar in conversation and then both men headed for Millar's office and left the party. At that point, Donna appeared with his beer.

"Here you go," she said, handing it to him. "Where did Pat go?"

"He left with your uncle. They should be back shortly."

"While they're gone do I get a birthday kiss?" she asked. Without waiting for him to reply, she stood on her toes and pecked him on the mouth. "We can do better another time," she added.

"Donna, not in front of everybody," he scolded her.

"Oh, who cares? It's my party. Why were you so late?"

"I had some business to take care of."

"With Cora Beth?"

"You don't even know who Cora Beth is, Donna, so why do you keep mentioning her?"

"She's my rival."

"You don't have a rival."

"You mean you're all mine?"

"I'm all *mine*, and you're a very young girl."

"I'm a woman, or didn't I prove that to you, already?" she asked, smiling suggestively.

"You're also a naughty young girl and you still need a good spanking," he told her.

"If that's an offer, I accept."

"You're just bad," he said. And she smiled coyly.

"How long are you going to be in Lancaster, Clint?"

"Why?"

"I'd just like to know so I can make plans."

"What kind of plans."

"For us, silly. If you're going to be here awhile, we can take our time, but if you're leaving soon, we'll have to make every second count."

"I'm sorry to disappoint you, Donna, but as far as I'm concerned, there is no *us* for us to make the most of."

"Clint—"

"Excuse me," he said as he noticed Pat return.

without Millar. He started across the room and caught Pat as he was going out the door.

"Pat, where are you going?"

"Back to town, like I told you."

"We were going to go back together," Clint reminded him. "What happened?"

"What happened?" Pat repeated. "I asked him for help, just like you suggested."

"And?"

"And he said no."

"No? Why not?"

"He said he'd already approached his men, and none of them would volunteer to stand with me against the Chamberses."

"He'd already asked them?"

"Yes. He said he asked them right after you came to see him about it."

"Oh."

"Hell, Clint, I'm not mad that you came to see him, but I can't understand why he said no. His men would do it if he wanted them to, I know they would."

"Maybe if I spoke to him again?"

"Forget it, Clint, just forget it. Let's go back to town and make our plans for the defense of it, and its ungrateful people."

"Pat—"

"Clint, I asked and he said no. Let's leave it at that."

Clint was stunned, to say the least. He had been so sure that Millar's hands would give them the help they needed, and now that it was just the two of them. . . .

"All right, Pat," he said. "Let's get back to town and make our plans. We'll use the saloon as our base.

Who knows, before long we may need a good stiff drink.''

"But just one," Pat said, and when Clint looked at him the young lawman said, "Lesson two, remember?"

TWENTY-FIVE

The saloon was still open when they got back to town, but the poker game had long since broken up.

"How'd the game come out?"

"The others quit before the stranger did. He took more off of them than you did."

"I told them to be more careful about who they played with," Clint said. "Give us each a whiskey, will you, Charlie, and then put on a pot of coffee. This may be an all-night session."

"What kind of session?"

"We've got to make our plans for when the Chambers gang gets here," Pat said.

"How many men did you get?"

Clint pointed a finger at Pat, then at Charlie, and then at himself.

"That's it?"

"That's it."

"What happened with the Millar crew?"

"No volunteers."

Charlie took out another glass and poured three whiskies, which they all promptly downed.

"That's it," Clint said. "Put the bottle away and put up a big pot of coffee."

"I'll make some sandwiches too. Somebody might get hungry."

"Close up early, will you, Charlie?" Clint asked.

"Sure."

When the coffee was made they all sat at a table and Pat and Charlie listened while Clint talked. "Ideally I'd like to have a man stationed north, south, east and west of town. We can't do that, so since there are three of us, two of us will have to position ourselves at points north and south."

"Why north and south?" Charlie asked.

"Those are the two roads leading into and out of town," Pat pointed out, but then he turned to Clint and asked, "Why should we assume they'll come in that way?"

"There's at least a dozen of them coming, right?"

"That's what we've heard."

"Exactly, that's what we've heard. Why have we heard that? Because they have not made it a secret that they are on their way here to Lancaster. Since they want everyone to know they're coming, why would they sneak into town?"

"You figure they'll come riding in on one of the main roads?"

"Right."

"Can't we figure on either north or south?"

"That depends on where they cross the border from New Mexico into Texas. We have no way of knowing that."

"Okay, so one of us is north and one of us is south of town," Charlie said. "Where's the other one?"

"In town, sitting on a porch or something, but somewhere where he'll see either of the others come riding into town with the word."

"Then what do we do?"

"Then we've got to get the man who's at the other

end and all gather together in the middle of town, where the bank is.''

"They're coming to burn us out, not rob us," Charlie said. "At least that's what I heard."

"It's all part of the same thing," Clint said. "If they destroy this town they're not going to just leave without touching the bank or some of the other stores. Block said they'd start with the jail, but I think they'll start at the bank."

"Why?"

"Well, once they get started taking the town apart some of the townspeople might get insulted and start shooting at them. This way, if that happens, they'll already have the money from the bank."

"You know," Charlie said, "I'm just starting to understand what this all means."

"This is deadly serious business, Charlie," Clint said.

"I believe it," the bartender said. "Excuse me, but I've got some things to do," he added, getting up.

"Like what?"

"Like waking up the mayor and the other members of the town council and having an emergency meeting. There's got to be something we can do about getting help, even if the council itself has to arm themselves."

"Good luck," Clint said, with feeling.

"Help yourselves to whatever you want," Charlie said before letting himself out and locking the door behind him.

"Think he'll have much luck?" Pat asked.

"I don't think we should count on it."

"What's next, then?"

"Dynamite."

"What about it."

"Is there any in town?"

"I guess so—I don't know. I guess we can find out."

"Assuming we get some," Clint went on, "we'll have to dig some holes in the road at the south end of town, and then cover them up sloppily, so that they're obvious enough to see from a distance with a pair of binoculars."

"How much dynamite do you want in each hole?"

"None."

Pat frowned and said, "Then what do you want us to put in the holes?"

"Nothing."

"Wait a minute. You want us to dig holes, then cover them up without putting anything in them?"

"That's right."

"At the south end of town."

"Right again."

"I don't understand this."

"You will," Clint assured him, "after I tell you what I want you to do at the north end of town."

TWENTY-SIX

In the morning there was another emergency meeting of the town coucil, and both Clint and Pat Garrett were invited to attend.

"I don't know what good this is going to do," Pat said as they walked to the town hall. "I've talked to all of these men individually already."

"Maybe Charlie was able to talk some sense into them," Clint proposed.

"We'll see."

When they entered the meeting room all eyes fell on them and Mayor Gault rose from the head of the table.

"Take seats, gentlemen, please," he invited.

They looked at each other, then moved forward to take two chairs next to each other. Across the table from them sat Charlie Anderson, looking grim.

"Charlie doesn't look too happy," Pat muttered to Clint, who silently agreed.

For a man in his seventies, Mayor Gault certainly did not look as if he were attending his second emergency council meeting in a matter of hours.

"Sheriff Garrett, I am given to understand that you are somewhat disappointed in the people of this town."

"I am, Mayor."

"Why?"

"None of them—none of you—will lift a hand to save your own town."

"That's what we pay *you* for," one of the council members said. Their names were unknown to Clint, but they didn't matter. They were all interchangeable as far as he was concerned.

"So I've been told," Pat said.

"None of us here are gunmen," Mayor Gault pointed out.

"Maybe not," Charlie Anderson said louder than necessary, "but I'll be standing with the sheriff, and with Clint Adams, when the Chambers gang comes to burn this town to the ground."

"Good for you," one of the others said. "We'll dig your grave before we move on."

"You're all so willing to just give up and move on to another place, start all over again?" Pat asked. "This town and the time you've put into it don't mean anything to you?"

"Pat, I've talked to these good people until I'm blue in the face," Charlie Anderson said, standing up, "and now I want nothing more to do with any of them."

He moved towards the door and left, slamming it behind him.

Clint stood up and looked at each of the six remaining council members in turn.

"That man," he finally said, pointing to the door that Charlie Anderson had just gone through, "is going to die because none of you have the guts to stand up for what's yours. I have more respect for Willy Chambers and his gang than I do for any of you."

With that Clint turned and walked out the door in the wake of Charlie Anderson.

Clint found Charlie standing right outside the building, leaning against a wooden post, absolutely fuming.

"I've never gotten that angry in my life, Clint," he said as the Gunsmith came up next to him.

"I guessed that, Charlie."

"What's wrong with them?"

"Nothing," Clint answered. "Charlie, lawmen were invented by people who were too afraid to take care of themselves, so they pay someone else to do it for them. That someone else is not supposed to ask them to help themselves. That just isn't done."

"And you accept that?"

"I did," Clint said, "but if I still did, I'd still be wearing a badge."

Charlie looked behind them and asked, "Where's Pat?"

"He's still inside."

"He's stubborn."

"But he's coming around."

"Should we wait for him?"

"Are you going to open today?"

"How can I open and defend the town at the same time?"

"All right. Why don't you go and see if you can find me some dynamite, and I'll wait for the sheriff."

"Right. How much do we need?"

"All we can get, Charlie."

Clint waited there for Pat, who came out after about five or six minutes.

"This is all up to you now, Pat," Clint told him. "You want to pull out, or stay?"

"What about you?"

"You're wearing the badge."

"For now," Pat replied. "I'm going to stay, Clint, but you don't have—"

"We went through that already, Pat."

"Okay," Pat said. "Thanks. Where did Charlie go, to open up the saloon?"

"He's not opening today. He went to get the dynamite. What about the council? Will they go along with our plan?"

"Are you kidding? All they have to do is stay off the streets. They were planning on doing that anyway."

"Then we're all set. Let's go over to the hardware store and get some shovels. We've got holes to dig."

TWENTY-SEVEN

At the hardware store they bought two shovels and a hoe and carried them to the saloon, where Charlie opened the doors to let them in.

"Did you get the dynamite?" Clint asked.

"A couple of dozen sticks was all they had."

"It'll do."

"Should we go and dig the holes now?"

"We've got something else to consider first."

"What?" Pat asked.

"John Stud."

"What about him?"

"It's too much of a coincidence that he's here. I think we should face the possibility that he may have been sent here in advance by the Chambers gang."

"And we don't want him to see what we're doing," Pat said. "What do you suggest?"

"Charlie, can you get someone to mind this place for you today?"

"Sure, I've got a couple of people I use when I want a day off."

"Get someone."

"What have you got in mind?" Pat asked.

"Stud is bound to come here for a drink, or a game of cards. I propose to keep him here while you dig your holes at one end of town, and Charlie digs his at the other."

"How are you going to keep him here?"

"Stud and I have a few things in common," Clint said. "I'm sure I'll be able to find something to talk about. As soon as you see me sit down with him, you've got to move."

"We'll move, don't worry," Charlie said.

"Then the first thing we have to do is open this place up."

"I'll be back in ten minutes with my man," Charlie said. "He's always looking for a few dollars and he won't refuse."

"Good. Pat, let's get this stuff over to the jail. We don't want Stud to see it lying around here."

"Right."

Pat carried the carton of dynamite while Clint carried the shovels and the hoe. When they got to the jailhouse, they put everything into one of the cells and then sat down to discuss some last-minute details.

"Clint, if Stud is involved, one of us is going to have to deal with him sooner or later."

"I think it should be me, Pat, and I hope you're not going to be stubborn about this."

"No," Pat said, shaking his head. "I was figuring it should be you, too. I'm nowhere near as good as you are with a gun."

"Now you're learning to think like a lawman," Clint said.

"Yeah, but there's one more thing."

"What's that?"

"Can you take Stud in a gunfight?"

"Maybe we won't have to find that out," Clint said, and when he saw that that statement did nothing for the young lawman's confidence, he added, "For his sake."

TWENTY-EIGHT

Clint went over to the saloon and left Pat at the jail. Clint told Pat he'd send Charlie over to let him know as soon as Stud came to the saloon, and they could get to work.

When he got to Charlie's place he found the bartender behind the bar with another man.

"You better get out from behind there, Charlie," he advised. "When you leave I don't want Stud to notice anything. He might get suspicious."

"Where do you want me, then?"

"Well, I guess you'll have to stay hidden in the back room. When Stud comes in your friend here—"

"Sam."

"—can let you know. You'll slip out the back way and go to the jail. Pat will let you know what to do next."

"Can you keep Stud talking for along?"

"Dig fast, and I won't have to. Oh, before you leave let me have a deck of cards. Maybe I can interest him in some two-handed poker."

"I'm in for half," Charlie said, reaching under the bar and handing him a sealed deck of cards.

"You're on." He turned to Sam and said, "I'll be sitting at that corner table. When the man we want comes in I'll nod to you and you let Charlie know.

Aside from that, all you have to do is tend bar as usual. Okay?''

"Yes, sir."

"Clint," Charlie said, "what if he doesn't come in here at all today?"

"Then we'll just have to do our digging by moonlight," Clint answered. "Starting tomorrow morning, we can begin to expect the Chambers gang at a moment's notice."

"That's encouraging."

"Well, the sooner we get it over with, the better, Charlie, however it goes."

"I suppose you're right."

"I think we have some time before we can start expecting Stud to want a drink," Clint said. "I'm going to my boardinghouse to get my gear and stow it in the jail. See you shortly."

"What if he comes in while you're not here?"

"Then serve him, but it's a little early for whiskey or beer, isn't it?"

"I hope so."

"Don't worry, I'll be back soon."

Clint left the saloon and walked to the boardinghouse. He went directly to his room for his rifle and saddlebags. While he was there Laura Dean stopped by the room.

"You're leaving?" she asked.

"Just moving for a while."

"To where?"

"The jail."

"What did you do?"

"Nothing. I promised to give a friend lawman lessons."

"Clint," she said, touching his arm, "is it true that

the Chambers gang is coming to Lancaster, and that you and the sheriff will be fighting them alone?''

"Unless you can think of someone who will stand with us," he told her. "We've tried every so-called man in town and in the surrounding ranches, without any luck."

"You've tried the men," she said. "Now how about trying the women?"

"What?"

"I can shoot a gun, Clint. I'll fight with you."

He stopped packing his saddlebags to turn around and look at her and see if she was serious.

"I'm serious," she said, as if reading his mind.

"That's a very courageous offer, Laura—"

"I said I'm serious, Clint," she broke in. "I'm not like the rest of the people in this town. This house is all I've got, and if I lose it I've got nowhere else to go."

"I can appreciate that," Clint said, "but I can't let you stand out there—" He stopped himself then as a thought occurred to him. "How well can you shoot a rifle?"

"Very well," she said, firmly. "I hit what I aim at."

"Okay," he said. "Okay. I may have something for you to do. Do you have a rifle?"

"I've got an old Henry—"

"I'll supply you with a better gun," he said. "But you have to be ready to move at a moment's notice."

"All right."

"Wear trousers, and do something with your hair so it doesn't fly into your eyes at the wrong moment."

"What will I be shooting at?"

"Something the size of one of your dinner plates, and probably from the roof of a two-story building."

"I'll be ready."

"You shouldn't find yourself in any immediate danger, Laura," he said, "but just the same, you'll have to keep your head down."

She nodded, and rubbed her upper arms with her hands, as if she was cold.

He put his hands over hers and said, "Honey, if you change your mind just let me know."

"I'm not going to change my mind, Clint," she assured him. "Not with you out there risking your life for my home."

He gathered her into his arms and held her close, and she slid her arms around his waist.

"You're special," he said. "You know that?"

"Show me," she said, looking up at him. "Please, show me how special you think I am."

He bent his head and kissed her, and her mouth opened hungrily beneath his.

"Please . . ." she said against his mouth.

He took his saddlebags from the bed and dropped them to the floor, and their clothes swiftly followed. Without turning down the covers they tumbled onto it, locked together in a frantic embrace. She was clawing at him, begging him to enter her and he did, quickly and brutally. She gasped and locked her limbs around him and there was a kind of savagery to the way she was grinding her hips against him.

"Oh God, yes, Clint, yes, I need it, please, don't stop . . ."

He had no intention whatsoever of stopping until they were both finished. With the Chambers gang possibly within arm's reach, and the prospect of facing them virtually alone, he needed this release almost as much as she did.

He began to drive her into a frenzy by drawing himself almost totally out of her, and then biting and sucking her nipples before driving himself into her again. He did this over and over until suddenly she began to shudder and buck beneath him. He drove himself deep inside her then and released the control he'd been holding over himself and began to shudder himself.

"God," she said forcefully as he emptied into her, and he wondered why so many women called out like that during sex.

"Oh, I needed that," she said. "I think I hate you a little because of how much I've been needing you since last time."

He didn't bother to point out that maybe it wasn't him she was needing, but simply sex.

"We're good together," he said.

"Yes, we are," she agreed, sitting up. "Now maybe you ought to go and do what you've got to do to get ready to save this town."

"I guess so."

As he was dressing she said, "Clint?"

"Yes?"

"Were you serious about using me, about letting me help?"

"Laura, honey," he said, picking up his rifle and saddlebags, "I can't afford not to be."

TWENTY-NINE

"One more day and we'll be there," Willy Chambers told his three brothers.

"Tomorrow morning?" Matt asked. "We could make it by late this evening easy. In fact, we could have been there by now."

"I think what the kid wants to know, Willy," Seth said, "is why are we taking so long in getting there?"

"And where's Stud?" Matt piped in.

"You boys better start breaking camp," Willy said, dumping the remnants of his morning coffee into the fire, rising and walking away.

"I don't think you guys asked him right," Rob Chambers said. "Let me take a shot."

Rob got up and followed Willy while the other two brothers went about breaking camp.

"Will," Rob said, coming up on his brother from behind.

"You got demands too?"

"No demands, Will," Rob said. "I just think we deserve to know why we're draggin' our asses."

Willy turned and looked at his brother for a few moments, then said, "You're a little smarter than the others, aren't you, Rob?"

"Don't put them down, Will," Rob said. "They're your brothers."

"Yeah. Okay, I sent Stud ahead to scout Lancaster and see if the Gunsmith is really there, like those two drifters said."

"Do you think one man would make that much of a difference?" Rob asked.

"This man would."

"Do you think Stud can take him out?"

"I don't want Stud to do anything but let me know if he's actually there. Lancaster's no different from any other town, Rob. When they hear that we're coming, they won't lift a finger to help. There's only going to be a sheriff, and maybe the Gunsmith."

"No deputies?"

"Have you ever known Lancaster to have any deputies? All it's ever needed was a sheriff, and not a very good one, at that."

"Then Gunsmith or not, this is going to be easy."

"A lot easier without him, Rob," Willy said. "A hell of a lot easier without him."

THIRTY

John Stud slid from bed without waking the girl next to him and walked to his hotel window. He had slept in late—well, truth be told he had not actually been sleeping—and it was almost noon. Looking at the main street of Lancaster he found it oddly deserted, but then the town must have known about the Chambers gang by now. Not knowing when they were going to show up, he didn't blame the people for staying indoors.

Turning to look at the naked young girl in his bed, he didn't think staying indoors was such a bad idea for him, either.

He went back to the bed and put his hand on the girl's behind and she stirred as he squeezed her right buttock, exerting more and more pressure until she squealed, came awake and struggled to get away from his grip.

"No!" she cried out, rolling over as he released, and covering her face with both hands.

"Come on now, little lady," Stud said, to her. "The damage isn't that bad, and I'll bet you even enjoyed it."

"Parts of it," she admitted, but then she dropped her hands away from her face so he could see the black eye he'd given her—in the heat of passion—and said, "But not this."

"Oh," he said, reaching out and touching the

bruise, ''I think I've got something to make you feel much better.''

She watched as he dropped his pants to the floor and revealed to her a raging erection, red and pulsating furiously.

The girl's name was Lottie and, at nineteen, she had been selling herself for the past four years to customers of the hotel, with the rat-faced clerk taking half of what she made on ''appointments'' that he set up. She was on the thin side, but she had very large breasts, which Stud had liked immediately, and on the right one were the bruised imprints of his fingers. He had no doubt that in a few hours she'd be wearing the same bruises on her right buttock.

Stud had fucked her at least half a dozen times during the night, from the front and from behind, and during one passionate moment had backhanded her viciously, just to add to his own thrill. The result of that blow was the black eye she now sported.

Now, as sore as she was between her legs, he was ready to go again and she had to submit, or not get paid, and she had already submitted to too much to give up the money she had coming.

Stud climbed on the bed, pushed her down on her back and entered her, driving his massive penis inside of her like a battering ram.

''Oh, God!'' she shouted, but only half in pain. The other half was sheer pleasure. Stud started driving into her and in spite of herself she was reacting, coming again and again in response to the stimulus of his massive cock. When he had first stripped she'd been shocked at the size of him. Physically he was not a large man, but when aroused his penis swelled to enormous proportions. It frightened her at first, but it was fright mixed with wonderment, and then when he entered her it became pure joy and passion and her reactions were very uncharacteristic of a prostitute.

On the other hand, to Stud the girl was just a receptacle for his need to impress himself. Even when he was having sex with a woman, it was not for her enjoyment, or his, but to impress himself. He marveled at their reactions when they first saw how well-endowed he was, and then he gloried in their joy when he entered them because it made him feel powerful, and in control—as he was now.

Straddling Lottie, he reached down and took a breast in each hand.

"No," she whimpered, knowing what he was going to do, but he did it anyway, squeezing and twisting her breasts, giving her pain and pleasure at the same time. As he felt himself swelling inside of her, preparatory to ejaculating, he brought his hand up and struck her across the face on the other side, driving her head into the pillow, and then exploded into her. When she screamed he knew it was a scream of pleasure, of joy, and as his seed pumped furiously into her his entire body seemed to swell with pride. She writhed beneath him, totally without control over her own body because of him.

She was writhing the way some of his victims writhed, especially when they were gut shot. The feeling he had then was just like the feeling he had now, of immense pride.

At that very moment he felt his head swell and it was as if it would explode if he didn't do something—if he didn't kill someone! He reached out and closed his hands around her throat and her eyes widened as she sensed what was about to happen.

"No!" she cried out. "Please!"

He continued to squeeze until her protestations were

trapped in her throat as unintelligible gurglings.

Then he let her go.

"No," he said as she took great, gulping breaths. "Not now, and not you." He withdrew from her and stood up, his erection still pulsing as he stood over her, feeling ten feet tall, and repeated, "Not you, little one."

THIRTY-ONE

"It's getting late," Pat Garrett said, looking at the clock in his office that read almost five.

"Yeah," Clint replied glumly. "I never realized that just sitting in one place for so long could be so tiring."

He stood up from his chair by the window and stretched his arm and back muscles.

"Pat, I think I'm going to go over and sit in the saloon. Maybe I could at least get up a game of poker while I'm waiting."

"I guess I'll just wait here," the lawman said. "I feel sorry for Charlie, waiting in the back room all this time."

"I feel sorry for all of us, but if nothing happens today, the odds become that much better that it will happen tomorrow."

"Seems to me they should have been here before now," Pat said.

Clint moved his chair away from the window and said, "That may be deliberate, Pat. If they did send Stud ahead to scout around, then they're taking their time, giving him an opportunity to evaluate our position."

"Doesn't take much to see that our position is grim."

''I can't argue that,'' Clint said. ''But we'll do our best to see that it gets better.''

''Can't get much worse.''

Clint just nodded and said, ''See you in a while. If he doesn't show by late tonight, we'll do our moonlight digging.''

When Clint walked into the saloon he was just in time to see Charlie Anderson's head pop out of the back room. The hopeful look on Anderson's face was almost comical. Clint decided to stop back there before taking a table.

''What's up?'' Charlie asked. ''Where is he?''

''As far as we know, he's still in his hotel.''

''Then this isn't going to work,'' Charlie exclaimed nervously.

''Take it easy, Charlie,'' Clint said. Looking around the room all he could see were boxes and crates of all sizes and shapes. ''I know it isn't easy sitting in one place all the time. I was going stir-crazy at the jail.''

''Yeah, it does get a little close in here after a while,'' Charlie admitted.

''I'm going to sit outside for a while and play some cards. If he doesn't come in pretty soon, we'll go out and dig our holes in the dark.''

''Good. I'd rather be out digging holes than cooped up back here.''

''It shouldn't be too much longer, Charlie.''

''Clint,'' the bartender said as the Gunsmith turned to leave.

''Yeah?''

''What if we're wrong? What if Stud has no connection with the Chambers gang.''

''If he doesn't, that would mean that there were only two other possibilities to explain why he is here.''

"What are they?"

"It's either coincidence, or he's looking for me,"
the Gunsmith said. "And I don't believe in coincidence."

THIRTY-TWO

When Clint left the back room he spotted Red and the other two poker players sitting at their regular table.

"You boys mind if I sit in and give you a chance to get your money back?"

Red looked up nervously and said, "Oh, you don't have to worry about that, Clint—"

"Come on, Red," Clint said. "I can assure you that I'm not a sore loser. Easy come, easy go, you know? I'm just looking to kill a little time."

He looked at the other two players, who nodded, and then said, "All right, sit yourself down."

Clint sat and they began to play. His mind was not on the game, so he lost regularly, which only made the other players more nervous.

When darkness had fallen totally and Clint had lost almost twenty dollars, he said, "Well, that's about it, boys. You've made half your money back, I think."

"Just about, Clint," Red said. "I'd say thanks, but you weren't really paying attention to the game. Were you letting us win?"

"No, Red," he answered. "I've just got something else on my mind, that's all. See you guys."

Clint left the table and went into the back room to get

Charlie. He found him sitting on a crate with his fist under his chin.

"Okay, pal, let's go. We've got some digging to do."

"At last," Charlie said, getting up quickly. "I feel like I'm getting out of prison."

"We'll go over to the jail, get Pat and our tools and get started on our holes."

"As long as I don't end up in one of them," Charlie said.

John Stud had left town just before dark, to meet Willy Chambers at a prearranged place outside of town. When he got there he found a dilapidated house and remnants of an old barn.

"This used to be my home," Willy Chambers said, coming out of the house.

Showing no sign of surprise Stud said, "That must have been a long time ago."

"Not long enough," Willy said. "I can still remember it."

"Are we gonna talk about your childhood?" Stud asked.

"Not much to talk about. Why don't you get down from your horse. I made some coffee inside."

Stud dismounted and tied off his horse, then followed Willy into what was left of the house.

"What have you been able to find out?" the oldest Chambers brother asked when he and Stud both had a cup of coffee in their hands.

"Not much," Stud said. "The Gunsmith is in town, all right. Those drifters were telling the truth about that."

"Did you see him?"

"I saw him."

"Does he know who you are?"

"Not by sight, but if he checked the hotel register he does."

"Do you think he did?"

"Either him or the sheriff."

"Who's the sheriff?"

"Fella named Pat Garrett, a young fella."

"I never heard of him."

"Adams seems to be guiding him, teaching him the ropes."

"Is Adams wearing a badge?"

"Not that I could see."

"Any deputies?"

"Nope."

"Then it's only the sheriff and Adams to stand against us, and they'd be fools if they tried."

"They'll try," Stud said confidently.

"What makes you say that?"

"You don't get a rep like the Gunsmith's by backing away from a fight, no matter how big the other guy is."

"Well, it doesn't matter," Willy said. "He's only one man."

"Sure."

"The sheriff hasn't been able to get any of the townspeople to stand with him, has he?"

"Not that I know of."

"He won't," Willy said, firmly. "That's what they pay him for."

"When are you coming in?" Stud asked.

"Tomorrow."

"Yes, but when?"

"Just be ready," Willy told him, emptying his coffee cup. "When we hit, you'll know."

"It'll be easier than you think," Stud said, doing the same.

"Why?"

Standing up Stud said, "I figure Adams will be keeping a close eye on me until you hit, so when you do, I'll take care of him."

"Are you sure you can outshoot him?"

Stud gave Willy Chambers a cold, level stare and said, "I can outshoot anybody."

Stud rode back into town from the south. The full moon enabled him to see that there was someone in the street, apparently digging. He couldn't see who it was well enough to identify them, but he was able to tell that it was neither the sheriff nor the Gunsmith. Still, what would someone be doing digging holes in the street in the middle of the night?

Stud turned his horse so that he could circle to the west and come into town that way. While he was riding, he wondered what he would be doing to prepare for the Chambers gang if he was the sheriff or Clint Adams that would involve digging holes in the ground. It didn't take him very long to decide what he would do; if Adams was doing the same thing, Willy Chambers and his brothers might be in for a little surprise.

If they came into town from the south, that is.

THIRTY-THREE

"Fill in the last hole, Pat, and then we'll use the hoe to smooth out the dirt." Clint got up from his knees and backed away so that Pat Garrett could fill the hole in.

"Do you think Charlie's done by now?"

"When we're finished we'll go and help him, then we'll all go and have a drink and then get some sleep."

"Did you ever work on a farm?" Clint asked Pat.

"Yeah, why?"

"Prior experience," Clint said. "Here, you hoe."

"Thanks."

Pat went over all of the holes they'd dug and then stepped back and said, "How's that?"

"Well, I've only got moonlight to judge by, but as far as I'm concerned, you'd never know that anybody had dug up the street."

"Good, let's go get Charlie and have that drink."

They started towards the south end of town on foot and came up on Charlie Anderson while he was filling in his last hole.

"Finished, Charlie?" Pat asked.

"Almost."

They watched as he dropped the last shovelful of dirt into the hole, then stamped it down with his boot.

"Finished," he said. "How does it look?"

In the moonlight Clint and Pat could clearly see

about eight patches of dirt that had been badly refilled. In fact, the holes were now higher than the rest of the street.

It was as sloppy a job of refilling as they had ever seen.

"It's perfect, Charlie," Clint said, patting the man on the back, "just perfect."

When they got to the saloon they went right to the bar and Charlie asked Sam, "Did he ever show up?"

Sam shook his head and said, "Nobody who looked like what you described to me showed up at all."

"What's his story, then?" Charlie asked, turning to Clint and Pat Garrett.

"Who knows?" Clint said. "Maybe he found himself a girl and holed up for the entire day."

"The desk clerk at the hotel, Lenny—"

"The guy with a face like a rat?" Clint asked.

"That's him," Sam said. "He's got a couple of girls that he supplies for the guests of the hotel."

"That must be it, then," Clint said. "He knew they weren't coming in today, so he stayed inside all day and caught up on his, uh, sleep."

"Three beers, Sam," Charlie told his temporary bartender.

When they all had their beers Sam said, "The man you were looking for didn't come in, but somebody did come in looking for you, Mr. Adams."

"Oh? Who?"

"He's sitting over there," Sam said, inclining his head in the direction of a table.

They all turned and looked at the young man who was sitting at a back table nursing a beer.

"Know him?" Pat asked Clint.

"Yeah, I know him," Clint said. "He lives in my boardinghouse."

"What's he want with you?"

"I think I might know, but I hope I'm wrong," the Gunsmith said. "Pat, why don't you go and get some sleep; I'll see you in the morning. Charlie—"

"I've got to close up, but I'll let you out when you're finished," Charlie said.

"Fine."

"Sam," Charlie said, "go home. Can you work tomorrow?"

"Sure can."

"Good."

Clint took his beer and walked to the back table to talk with Bill Gaines—not, he hoped, about Cora Beth.

"Bill."

Gaines looked up and said, "Mr. Adams."

"I understand you're waiting for me?"

"Yes, that's right."

Clint sat down and saw that Gaines only had about an inch of beer left in his mug.

"Another beer?"

"Oh, no thanks," the young man said. "I don't drink much."

"All right. What did you want to see me about?"

The boy fiddled with his nearly empty mug nervously and Clint felt almost sure that he was trying to get up his nerve to fulfill his husbandly duties and confront Clint about Cora Beth.

"Look, Bill, maybe I can make this easier for both of us—" Clint started to say, but Gaines broke in without giving him a chance to finish.

"No, I don't want it to be easy," the kid said. He drank the remainder of his warm beer in one convulsive movement, then made a face and shuddered. "Look,

Mr. Adams, I talked to Mrs. Dean and she told me that you're getting ready for the Chambers gang to come to town.''

"That's right.''

"I want to fight with you.''

So, it wasn't about his young wife at all—or was it? "Can you shoot a gun, Bill?''

"Sure.''

"Do you own one?''

"No,'' he said, lowering his head. "I can't afford one.''

"What kind of a gun can you shoot?''

"A rifle.''

"Not a handgun?''

"I never had much need.''

"Can you shoot well?''

"Uh, not . . . very well, no—but I want to fight!''

"How old are you, Bill?''

"Twenty-two.''

"Anybody ever call you Billy?''

"Everybody . . . used to,'' he admitted.

"What happened?''

"Cora Beth. She said that only little boys are called Billy.''

"Why do you want to fight?''

"Be-because I live here,'' Bill Gaines said. "This is my home and I don't want to see it burned to the ground and looted.''

"I see.''

"Can I fight alongside you, Mr. Adams?''

Clint studied the boy, who seemed very determined and sincere about fighting.

"All right, Billy,'' Clint said. "You be ready to-morrow. Skip work and come to the livery stable at nine in the morning, and bring Mrs. Dean with you.''

"Thank you, Mr. Adams," the boy said, getting up from the table. "Thank you very much."

As Gaines started to walk away from the table Clint called out, "Billy."

"Yes?" the boy answered nervously.

"Does your desire to fight have anything to do with Cora Beth?"

Gaines looked at the floor and shuffled his feet, then looked back at Clint and started to say, "What would Cora Beth have to do with—"

"You wouldn't be trying to prove something to her, would you?" Clint interrupted.

He thought about it, and then answered, "Yeah, I might be—but I don't intend to get killed trying to do it."

Clint smiled and said, "Actually, Billy, none of us intends to get killed tomorrow."

"H-how many of us are there, exactly?"

"A few," Clint said. "A very few—but we'll make our presence known, don't worry about it. Go and get yourself some sleep. We've all got a big day tomorrow."

"You think it's going to be tomorrow?"

"Billy, I'm hoping it will be."

THIRTY-FOUR

Pat offered Clint one of the jailhouse's two cells to sleep in, but Clint said that he had some work to do in his wagon, and would therefore sleep in it.

In his wagon he went about choosing weapons for his additional volunteers, Laura Dean and Billy Gaines. For Laura he chose a Winchester '73, the only one he had in his stock. It had the advantage of not only shooting true, but often. The newest thing in repeating rifles, it had a reputation of being the finest weapon ever made. Clint's reason for giving it to Laura was so that even if she couldn't hit anything, she'd at least be able to fire quickly.

He had something else in mind for Billy Gaines, in whom he had less confidence with a rifle than he did in Laura Dean. At least he had admitted to not being able to shoot very well. He had a sawed-off Greener shotgun. There wasn't much chance of Gaines missing with that, and even when he did the pellets would still be able to strike the street, which would be just as good as hitting someone. The only drawback was that Gaines would have to be closer to the action than Laura, while still being in a position where he could shoot down at the gang. He hoped the kid would be up to it and not balk. Having two extra guns firing during the action would at least serve to confuse the enemy, who were probably expecting token resistance, at best.

That done, the Gunsmith turned his attention to his own weapons. His Springfield rifle and his modified Colt both fired .45 caliber bullets, so he had plenty of loads for each weapon. The revolver had been modified to be fired double-action; in other words, the Gunsmith did not have to cock the hammer on the gun to fire it, but merely had to pull the trigger. Consequently, the gun fired as fast as he could yank the trigger, which came in handy.

It had saved his life on more than one occasion.

With his weapons cleaned he began to set up his bed, which meant that he padded the wooden floor with a couple of blankets and folded up a third to use as a pillow. He often slept in the wagon on especially cold nights on the trail.

He had just about finished all of his chores when he heard one of the livery doors creak. Lancaster was a town that did not lock up its stable overnight, which didn't worry Clint all that much because he was able to lock up his own wagon, while Duke acted as an effective watchdog to protect the team. Whoever was now entering the stable did not necessarily know that he was in there, but if they didn't, then he was getting into the realm of coincidence again, and he'd already said many times what he thought of that.

As quietly as he could, he doused his lamp and opened the back door of the wagon.

"Clint," he heard somebody whisper. It was hard to tell with a whisper, but it sounded like a woman.

"Clint, it's Donna," the voice called out, and the Gunsmith reached back and turned up his lamp.

"There you are," she said, coming to the back door of the wagon.

"Come on in," he said, backing off so she could

enter. Once she was inside he locked the door again.

"My God," she said, as she looked around at all of the guns and related items that adorned the wooden walls of the wagon. "You really are a gunsmith, aren't you?"

"The more people that know that, the better," he said. "Especially the paying customers. Donna, what are you doing here?"

"I came to see you."

"Does your uncle know where you are this time?"

"No, but Uncle is used to that now. I'm growing up, you know."

"I know," he said. "From firsthand experience. You shouldn't be here, though."

"I'll bet you think I came here just to be with you again."

"I don't care why you came, young lady, but you're going back," he told her, moving to open the door again.

"I came to help," she said quickly.

"With what?"

"The Chambers gang."

Clint stopped short of the door and asked, "What do you know about the gang?"

"More than you do, I think," she said. She lowered herself to his bed of blankets and tucked her legs underneath her.

"All right, little lady, what do you know that I don't?"

"Sit here with me," she said, patting the blanket beside her.

He shrugged and gave in, sitting beside her.

"Now, what about the Chambers gang?"

"This is serious, Clint," she said, and adjusted her face to match her words. "I can tell you why my uncle wouldn't let any of his men volunteer to help you fight the gang.''

"Wouldn't *let* them?" Clint asked.

"Clint, he didn't even ask them."

"But he told me, and he told Pat—"

"He lied to both of you."

"Why?"

"You have to understand my uncle first," she said. "He came from a small family. There was just him and his parents, and his younger sister. Her name was Donna too, and he loved her very much."

"What does all of this have to do with—"

"Let me tell it," she asked, laying her hand on his arm. "My uncle loved his sister very much," she said. "Donna went on and had her own family, a large one." She looked at Clint and said, "She had four sons and a daughter. The birth of the daughter killed her."

"Wait a minute," he said, stopping her. "Are you trying to tell me—"

"Willy Chambers and his brothers are my brothers," she said. "My uncle won't send his men to fight his sister's sons."

THIRTY-FIVE

"Your brothers," he repeated, staring at her.

"That's right," she said, "and I know what you're thinking."

"What?"

"That tomorrow you'll be doing your best to try and kill them."

She was right, that was what he was thinking. "Donna—"

"Don't let it bother you, Clint," she said. "The youngest boy is almost eight years older than me. And he left town over ten years ago. I never knew any of them." She shifted to stretch her bare legs out in front of her. "My old man was a drunk, and when my mother died my uncle took me away from him so that he and Aunt Kate could raise me. I don't think anyone in town now knows I'm really a Chambers or remembers my mother. Uncle Ken did his best to protect me from gossip and my father never fought it. With the boys taking off as soon as they were old enough and without me, he had two hands free for the bottle instead of one."

"When's the last time you saw your father?"

"A long time ago. He never came out to the ranch, and if he had Uncle would have run him off. When he died it barely affected me."

"It affected your brothers, though."

"Willy maybe, not the others, and Willy probably bullied the others into riding with him."

"Is he the biggest as well as the oldest?"

"No, but from what Uncle Ken says, he's the smartest—but that wouldn't take very much."

"Donna, are you telling me that if we approached your uncle's men some of them would volunteer."

"I'm sure they would, Clint."

"Then come morning I'll have to send somebody out there to ask them," he said. It would have to be Billy Gaines. He didn't know if Laura could ride well enough—

"Let me do it, Clint."

He looked at her, saw that she was sincere—and she had to go back there, anyway.

"Okay, Donna, you're it."

"That means I'll have to spend the night here."

"Sleeping," he pointed out. "You can't ride all that way if you're tired."

She put her hand out and pushed it into his shirt between two buttons and began to massage his chest.

"The horse knows the way, Clint," she said. "Believe me."

"Where is your horse?" he asked her.

"Outside."

"I'll go out and get him, bring him inside and bed him down," he said.

"Good," she said. "Then you can come back and do the same for me."

"Behave," he told her.

She pouted at him and he left the wagon to tend to her horse.

Donna's explanation cleared up the mystery about why Millar all of a sudden couldn't give them any help, and it also meant things were looking up. If the Chambers gang would hold off just long enough for some of Millar's men to get to town, things might start looking a lot better.

He found her bay mare just outside the livery and walked her inside. He removed the saddle, rubbed her down, gave her some grain, then stopped at Duke's stall to check on the big Arabian gelding.

"How're you doing, big boy?" he asked, stroking the horse's massive neck. "I haven't been paying much attention to you this trip, have I?"

Duke shook his head, either in answer to the Gunsmith's question, or to shake loose a tick or a fly. Sometimes Clint thought that Duke was smarter than most people.

"Okay, partner, I got a little filly waiting for me in the wagon that I've got to put to sleep without letting her get her claws into me." He scratched his partner's head and said, "You don't have that problem, so maybe you're lucky. Then again," Clint said, thinking about some of the more memorable women he'd been with—Sara, J.T. Archer, Michele Bouchet—he said, "Then again, maybe you're not."

He walked back to the wagon and pulled open the back door. It was dark inside, the lamp having been turned way down.

"Donna?"

"Clint," the voice came out of the darkness, "I've made your bed for you." Then she giggled and added, "I've made it nice and warm."

I'll bet, he thought, climbing into the wagon and pulling the door closed behind him.

THIRTY-SIX

He woke up the next morning to the insistent pressure of her mouth and her tongue against his penis.

"I think it's dead," he said, looking down at the crown of her head.

"No, it's not," she said. She took it full into her mouth and began sucking, and it began to swell. She let it out of her mouth long enough to say, "See?" and then went back to work on it, until it exploded, filling her mouth.

When Pat Garrett arrived at the livery later that morning Clint was waiting for him outside the wagon while Donna was inside getting dressed.

"Sleep okay?" Clint asked.

"I guess. Are we ready?"

"We're waiting for the rest of our crew," Clint said. "Charlie, Laura Dean and Billy Gaines."

"Gaines?"

"The kid in the saloon last night."

"What are you going to do with the woman?"

"Put her on a roof with a repeating rifle at the north end of town. I'm going to do the same thing with the kid, with a shotgun."

"Can they hit what they shoot at?"

"All they have to hit is the ground."

"Clint, if they run out on you, you'll be alone until we can get there from the south end. Let us stay at the other end with you."

"You and Charlie have to stay at the south end, just in case our plan doesn't work and they come in that way."

"Clint—"

"Besides, we may have some more help—a lot more."

"From who?"

"The men from the Millar ranch."

"I told you—"

"Pat, did you know that the Chambers boys were Millar's nephews?" Clint asked.

"What?"

Clint went on and explained to the lawman everything that Donna had explained to him the night before.

"Where did you hear this from?"

"Donna Millar—although I guess her real name is Chambers."

"Donna? Where is she?"

"Inside."

"You're not going to use her, are you? She's just a kid—"

"She's going to ride back to the ranch and ask the men for volunteers."

"That won't put her in very good with her uncle."

"She doesn't think very much of her brothers and doesn't want to see them burn this town," Clint explained. "She's doing the right thing, and I think he'll understand."

"I hope so, for her sake," Pat said.

When Charlie Anderson arrived, they explained the situation to him.

"Well, then things are looking up," he said.

"We hope so," Clint replied.

"Here come the rest of our men," Pat said.

Billy Gaines came walking in with Laura Dean, just as Donna climbed out of the back of Clint's wagon. She was fastening the top buttons on her dress as her eyes caught Laura's, and the two women stared at each other for a few seconds.

"All right, listen up," Clint said. "Anybody who wants to change their mind can pull out now." Nobody said anything, so he went on to outline the plan and everyone's part in it. "Donna, you'd better get going. Charlie, saddle her horse for her."

"Right."

He turned to Billy and Laura and said, "I've got guns for you two." He climbed into the wagon and came out with the Winchester and the Greener. "This is for you, Laura," he said, handing her the Winchester. "Just keep firing it as fast as you can."

He handed the Greener to Billy Gains and said, "You'll be closer to the action than Laura will, Billy. Can you handle it?"

"I—I think so."

He would have liked the kid to be surer, but he was asking enough of him as it was.

"I'll be on the ground, in one of the storefronts. Just keep firing until I signal you to stop. Do you both have that?"

"Yes," Laura said, and Gaines nodded.

"She's ready to go, Clint," Charlie said.

Donna rode up alongside Clint and Pat. "Be careful," Clint told her, "and don't stop for anything."

"I won't."

"Donna."

"Yes, Pat?"

"Tell your uncle I—tell him I understand."

She smiled at him and said, "I'll tell him, Pat."

"All right," Clint said when she had ridden off. "We don't have time to waste. They could come in any minute now, so let's get into position."

"There's something I should mention," Charlie said.

"What's that?"

"On the way over here I saw Stud go into the café. He's probably having breakfast."

Clint didn't waste any time making a decision. "I think I'll go over and have a talk with him."

"What for?" Pat asked.

"He's either been in touch or will be in touch with the Chamberses," he answered. "Maybe I can tell him enough to make him think twice, and maybe he'll relay the word to Willy Chambers. I think we'd all prefer to avoid this confrontation altogether, wouldn't we?"

"*We* would," Pat said, indicating all the people gathered in the livery. "But what about them?"

"Let me see what I can do about that right now."

THIRTY-SEVEN

When Clint entered the café John Stud was the only customer there having breakfast. The gunman was seated at a back table with his back against the wall.

"Mind if I have a seat?" Clint asked. He was confident that Stud had already made it his business to spot him, and knew who he was.

"Help yourself," Stud said. "I was wondering when we'd get around to this conversation."

"Well, I've been a little busy," Clint said, taking a seat.

"I've noticed," Stud answered. "Coffee?"

Clint waved at the waitress for another cup, and then poured it full from Stud's pot.

"No doubt you're wondering why I'm here," Stud said.

"Well, I've eliminated coincidence. You're either here for me, or you're an advance man for the Chambers gang."

Stud smiled and said, "How about both?"

"Yeah," Clint said, thinking, "how about that?"

"I've noticed that you've been having trouble getting men to stand with you and the young sheriff."

"It's been a problem," Clint admitted.

"So the two of you are going to stand alone?"

"We've made some plans to even the odds."

"Yes, I've noticed that too."

"Just what have you noticed?"

"I saw a man digging holes in the street at the south end of town, last night."

"I don't know anything about that," the Gunsmith said, quickly.

"Oh, come on, Mr. Gunsmith. You know, I did some thinking about what I'd do if I was in your position."

"And what did you come up with?"

"I'd dig some holes," Stud said, smiling, "and fill them with dynamite."

"What good would that do?"

"Stop playing dumb, Adams," Stud said, dropping his smile and replacing it with a scowl. "You could fire into the ground and explode the dynamite in their path. Well, after breakfast I'm going to take a ride out and see Willy Chambers and let him know about the holes. That is, unless you want to stop me."

Clint hoped he looked as if he was considering it.

"Sooner or later we'll face each other," Stud went on. "But if it's now and you lose, those people you've got out there are going to be without a leader. Think about it. It's your choice."

Clint frowned into his coffee cup.

"I'm going to get up now and walk over to the door, then I'm going to the livery to get my horse. You've got that long to make up your mind, Mr. Gunsmith."

Stud stood up slowly and Clint looked at him. The man had a smug, self-satisfied look on his face, probably pleased with himself that he had forced the Gunsmith to back down.

Clint hoped that everyone was out of the livery stable by now. He didn't want anything changing Stud's mind about riding out to meet and warn the Chambers gang about riding into Lancaster from the south.

Thanks to his warning, they'd come riding in from the north, where Clint Adams and his meager defense would be waiting for them.

Clint waited until he was sure Stud had plenty of time to ride out of town, then left the café and hurried on foot to the south end of town.

Pat and Charlie were properly placed on rooftops. He stood in the center of the street so that they'd be sure to see him, and then he tried to wave them down. Obviously puzzled, the two men hesitated and he was forced to wave them down a couple of more times before they finally complied.

"What's wrong?" Pat asked, with Charlie Anderson close behind him.

"Come with me," Clint said, starting off at a trot. "We've got to hurry to the other end of town."

"Why?" Pat asked.

"Stud saw Charlie digging the holes last night," Clint explained.

"That means—" Pat started, but Clint rushed on without giving him a chance to finish.

"That means that Stud is convinced that the best way for the Chambers gang to come into town is from the north."

"Then we have them!" Pat shouted.

"I hope so."

"Wait a minute," Anderson said. "What if they don't come in from the north? What if they still come in from the south?"

Clint looked at Pat, then looked at the panting, red-faced bartender and said, "In that case, they'll have us."

THIRTY-EIGHT

The setup was different now. Laura Dean was still placed up high, and Bill Gaines on a low roof. Clint was positioned inside a woman's clothing store. This was according to the original plan, but now Pat had been added in the storefront across the street, and Charlie Anderson had been stationed on a rooftop above Billy Gaines. The people on the rooftops were ordered to keep a very low profile, so that they could not be spotted by anyone scouting the town with a pair of binoculars.

As Willy Chambers was doing at that very moment.

"I can see the holes," he said to Stud, who was standing beside them.

"They had somebody out there last night digging in the dark."

"I guess they should have gotten themselves a farmer," Willy said. "He would have done a better job."

"Why they waiting for us at the south end?" Rob asked.

"They don't have enough people to cover both," Willy said. "They had to make a decision, and they had a fifty-fifty chance of being right."

"But now they'll be at the north end," Rob said,

"and we can come riding in from the south."

Willy lowered his binoculars and looked at his brother. "With dynamite buried in the street, brother, even one man on a rooftop with a repeating rifle can do a hell of a lot of damage. No, we'll come in from the north and ride right down the main street to the bank. First we'll take the money, then we'll set the buildings on fire. I want anyone who's in the street shot down."

"What if it's Uncle Ken?" Rob asked.

"He won't be there," Willy said firmly. "He won't fight against his dear sister's boys. Nope, we're dealing with three men, at most, one at the south end and two at the north end."

"What if they plant dynamite at the north end now?"

"Town that size ain't got that much dynamite," Willy said. "They'd have to dig it up from the other end and bring it down to this end and do it in a hurry. They might even blow themselves up doing it. No, they made their plans, now they're gonna have to stick by them."

"While we change ours, huh?"

"That's right. Rob, those two drifters still want to fight with us?"

"That's what they say."

"All right, cut 'em loose and give them their guns." As his brother started away Willy grabbed his arm and said, "When we're finished with the town, we're finished with them too. Understand?"

"I understand, Will."

"Okay, go."

Willy raised the binoculars again and stared down at the town he hated.

"Won't be long now," he said softly.

"Willy," Stud said, "I'm going to come in trailing behind you."

"Why?"

"I don't want to take a chance on catching a stray bullet."

Willy Chambers lowered his hands and looked at Stud. "Stud, you ain't afraid I'll backshoot you, are you?"

"I think you'd like it fine if everyone but you and your brothers was killed so you could keep the money in the family," Stud said. "And I ain't even that sure about your brothers. But no, that ain't what I'm worried about."

"Then what?"

"I've got business with the Gunsmith, and I think he'll be staying out of harm's way too, waiting for me."

"What do you want me to do with him if he kills you?"

"Willy," Stud said, "that's one problem you won't ever have to find out the answer to."

Where are they? the Gunsmith found himself wondering from inside the dress shop. *Are they going to let us stew awhile, or are they already riding in from the south end?* Had he made an error in judgment by placing everyone here?

He looked across the street again at Pat, who was waiting for the signal from Charlie Anderson so he could pass it on, but Pat just shook his head to indicate that there had been no signal yet.

Chambers wants us as nervous as he can get us, Clint was thinking. This whole situation reminded him of the time he, Wyatt Earp and Bat Masterson were holed up in a ghost town waiting for a gang of men to come riding in.* Then, a whole lot of luck—and the brothers of Bat and Wyatt—had seen them through.

I wonder if Pat has any brothers. . . .

Willy Chambers stood alone, staring down at Lancaster, Texas, the town of his birth and his father's death. He didn't know which event made him hate it more.

Let them sweat, he thought. *Let them know that we're out here, and wonder when we're coming in to destroy them, to wipe them off the face of the map.*

It won't be long now, Pa. Not long, at all.

John Stud made a decision.

He decided that once Willy and the rest of the men entered town from the north, and the shooting started, he'd enter from the south. Once in town, he'd await the outcome—which was hardly in doubt—and then go looking for Clint Adams.

He hoped he would find the Gunsmith alive—and then proceed to make that a very temporary condition.

The Gunsmith #5: Three Guns for Glory, Charter Books, May, 1982.

THIRTY-NINE

"All right, let's get this over with," Willy Chambers said. "Everybody mount up."

With the addition of the two drifters the Chambers gang now consisted of thirteen men. With only three men to face—one of whom would be at the other end of town when the shooting started—Chambers figured the odds were heavily in his favor. While they would actually be facing five gunhands, of varying skill, the odds were virtually the same.

"Ride slow," he ordered. "Nobody fires a shot unless I do, or unless we're fired at. Got it?"

Everyone had it, and the twelve of them started towards town with only one thought in mind—to destroy it.

John Stud sat astride his horse and watched as the dozen men worked their way down the hill towards town.

Don't get careless, Adams, he thought. *I'll be down soon enough, and I've got a bullet with your name on it.*

He began to circle so that he would come in from the opposite end, and he felt his entire body beginning to swell with need—but not merely the need to kill *some-*

body. This time, he was suffused with the need to kill one man: Clint Adams, the Gunsmith.

Clint Adams had been using the last twenty minutes to build himself a wall out in front of the store. He had found crates tightly packed with material, and it occurred to him that they would very effectively stop a bullet. He decided that instead of waiting inside he would pack the crates one on top of the other in front of the store, where he would be able to snap off much cleaner, clearer shots when the gang rode in.

Pat Garrett, seeing what Clint was up to, found crates of nails in the hardware store where he was stationed, and decided to do the same thing, so that by the time the signal came down from Charlie Anderson on the roof, he and Clint had built themselves some excellent cover from which to fire.

Since Clint and Charlie Anderson had dug the holes at this end of town, they knew approximately where they were. However, for the benefit of Laura Dean and Billy Gaines, the area had been marked off. A bale of hay had been set on the boardwalk to mark the beginning of the area, and another bale of hay had been set farther down the road where the area ended. Between these two markers was about twenty feet of open space, and it was when most of the gang was in that area that everyone was supposed to start firing—and not before. Any premature firing could ruin the whole plan. Clint hoped for the hundredth time that Gaines and Laura Dean were up to it.

When Anderson waved his arm at Pat, the lawman in turn waved at Clint, and things were just about to get started.

Clint leaned on top of his crate wall so that he could

peer down the street. His first indication that anyone was coming was the amount of dust that was being kicked up; then slowly, through the clouds of dust, he began to make out the shapes of men on horses.

Okay, he thought. *Here we go.*

Farther down the street, Mayor Gault was standing in front of his office. In his hands he had a notepad and a pencil, and he was determined to get as much of this down on paper as he could. He was a safe distance away so that he was in no danger from stray bullets, but he was close enough to see much of the action. He was sure that this story, with the famous Gunsmith as his main character, would be his finest work yet.

His publishers in New York would flip when they received the latest W.C. Gault epic:

CLINT ADAMS, THE GUNSMITH: THE TOWN SAVER.

> *The vicious Chambers gang, forty strong or more, rode down the main street of Lancaster, Texas, heavily armed to the man and showing no fear whatsoever at the prospect of facing that famed gunman and town saver known as The Gunsmith.*

The Chambers gang, all thirteen of them, were at best a ragtag-looking group, but Willy, riding in the lead, was certain that he had more than enough firepower to do the job.

The only members of his gang who knew they were going against the Gunsmith were his brothers, John Stud and the drifters, Wall and Fields. The other six men, all professional gunmen, would undoubtedly have heard of Adams, and he didn't want to take a chance on any of them running out. As it was, those six were a little shaky at the prospect of taking on an entire town.

> *Unafraid, and armed only with his revolver, The Gunsmith stood square in the center of the street, waiting for the gang to reach him. He had a small smile on his face, for he knew that even forty men were no match for his lightning speed and accuracy with a handgun. He stood alone waiting, and ready.*

Clint Adams was neither nervous nor calm. Being too much of either could always be fatal. He was wary and ready. He looked across the street at Pat and thought that the young man would make a fine lawman—if he survived this.

The men and horses were very clear now, and clustered as they were it was difficult to count, but he felt certain they were dealing with ten or twelve men at the most. He was certain of his and Pat's ability to fire effectively; he only hoped that the others weren't so bad that they wouldn't even be able to hit the ground.

> *Always careful to play fair, even when dealing with the basest of men, The Gunsmith was determined that he would not fire first. The gang would have to be the ones to first draw their guns and fire, after which they would fall prey to his matchless skill and courage.*

Clint had told Charlie not to wait for anything. As soon as the majority of the gang were positioned between those two hay markers, he was to start firing, and the others were to follow.

He watched as the lead rider passed the first bale of hay, keeping his horse at a walk. Behind came the others, now neither clustered or spread. Three, then five were past the first hay bail, then eight . . . and it was time.

Fire, he thought, but nothing happened. *Shit! Charlie, where are you? Fire! Fire!*

He looked across the street at Pat, who looked as puzzled as he was sure he himself did; Willy Chambers was approaching the second bale of hay and would soon be beyond that point.

Fire, damn it! Shoot!

He extended his arm and was about to fire at Chambers when he heard Charlie fire. He was able to identify the sound of the Winchester as Laura Dean fired, but so far their shots had no effect but to scatter the men. He fired and his shot ripped one man from his saddle. As the man fell his gun went off, firing into the ground and striking one bundle of buried dynamite.

With the explosion came total chaos.

Billy Gaines, who had been frozen with fear up to that point, was galvanized into action by the sound of the explosion. He stood up and pointed the shotgun down and pulled both barrels. The twin loads of buckshot spread out as they traveled and, by some miracle, did not strike a single man. They did, however, spread wide enough to strike the ground and set off two more explosions. Men shouted, thrown to the ground, and horses screamed and ran off.

Everyone was firing now. Willy Chambers and three or four men were still mounted, but the rest of the gang had been unseated by the dynamite explosions.

Pat fired at a mounted man and his shot knocked the man from his saddle, wounding him in the shoulder.

Seth Chambers staggered to his knees and began to look for something to shoot at. He saw Garrett just as Pat was about to fire again, and both men did so at the same time. Seth's bullet struck a carton of nails, imbedding itself harmlessly, while Pat's bullet literally tore the top of the man's head off.

Billy Gaines reloaded and blindly fired both barrels again. Some of the buckshot struck the ground harmlessly, failing even to set off a charge of dynamite, but a good portion of it punched Jeff Wall in the chest, shattering everything in its path and tearing his back out.

Some of Chambers's men were on their knees, firing up at the rooftops. Willy Chambers, Rob, and Billy Field were still astride their horses, firing at Clint and Pat.

Something Pat had not figured on when he set up his crate wall was a bullet entering one of the crates, striking the nails and giving off a spark which set the wood of the crate on fire. In a moment his barricade was a wall of flame and he had to move out from behind it. As he did so Billy Field spotted him and snapped off a shot, striking the lawman in the left arm, spinning him around and knocking him to the ground. At that moment a bullet from Laura Dean's rapidly firing Winchester struck a bunch of buried dynamite directly underneath Field's horse. The ensuing explosion lifted horse and rider off the ground and dropped them both down again, dead.

Rob Chambers was now on the ground on one knee, next to his brother Matt, and they were both firing at Billy's low roof.

Billy, having successfully loaded and fired several times, chose that inopportune moment to get brave. He stood up so that this time he could see what he was shooting at, and both Rob and Matt Chambers fired at him. Each slug caught Gaines in the chest and his fingers convulsively jerked on the triggers of the shotgun, firing the loads harmlessly into the air, and dropping the shotgun over the edge of the roof. He staggered about, his legs working reflexively, and then toppled over the edge of the roof after his weapon.

He was dead before he struck the ground.

FORTY

For all of the noise the dynamite had made, only three men lay dead as a result. One man was still mounted, the others were on the ground, their horses scattered by the dynamite. They began to scramble off the street for cover now, which rendered the remaining dynamite ineffective.

Clint looked for Pat and spotted him hunkered down behind a horse trough. He waved with his gun hand to indicate that he was all right, and Pat waved back.

At least the dynamite had served two purposes: It had stopped the gang from entering the center of town, and it had knocked them from their horses. The only man still mounted was the leader, and he now jumped down from his mount willingly and sought cover.

The initial engagement was now over, and half the gang lay dead in the streets, while The Gunsmith stood unscathed, calmly re-loading his six-gun.

Now it was simply a firefight, everyone shooting from cover. Clint had not seen Billy Gaines's body fall from the roof, but neither did he hear the sound of the shotgun any longer, which meant something was wrong.

Laura Dean kept firing her Winchester rapidly, although now she was almost totally ineffective. Charlie Anderson was not doing much better. Before long the gang would realize this and begin to work its way down to the only two men who posed a danger to them, Clint Adams and Pat Garrett.

Things had gone better than they might have expected up until that point, but not as well as they had hoped.

Willy Chambers was seething. This was Stud's fault. It was on his word that they had come into town this way, and they had been stopped. They were lucky that only three men lay dead in the street, although at that point he was unaware that one of them was his brother, Seth.

He looked around and found that his men were scattered, finding cover wherever they could. The fact that there was still firing coming from the roof told him that whoever was up there had no idea what they were doing.

That mean that there were only two people they had to deal with, Garrett and Adams.

And the odds were still five-to-one against *them*.

Damn it, Clint thought. *Why doesn't Laura stop firing? Doesn't she know there's nothing left to shoot at?*

No, of course she didn't know. She'd been told to keep firing, and that's what she was doing. She'd also discredited herself as any kind of a future threat. At least Charlie had the sense to stop firing when the gang took cover.

They wouldn't be under cover for very much longer, though.

For the first time he noticed a small buckboard across the street not far from where Pat was taking cover. It seemed to be loaded with supplies from the hardware store. How long had it been there? If the wagon had been there since yesterday, maybe there was some dynamite on it. He tried to get Pat's attention, and when he did he pointed to the wagon. The lawman nodded, turned and made a break for the wagon.

It was then that Clint noticed the blood covering Pat's left arm.

When Pat reached the wagon he climbed aboard. He was favoring his left arm, so he holstered his gun in order to be able to use his right. Once he was on the wagon he began to look around, moving things with his good hand. It looked like an order for one of the ranches and had probably been loaded in advance for future pickup. Pat thought he knew what Clint wanted, and he hoped it would be there.

There it was, in the midst of kegs of nails, barbed wire and shovels—a case of dynamite. Actually, it was too much for their purpose. If it all went off at once, it would take half the town with it, and their aim was to save the whole town, not reduce half of it to rubble.

With Clint covering him he quickly started dumping the nonessentials off the side of the wagon, then opened the case of dynamite and took some out. He slid the case with the remaining sticks down to the end of the wagon, got down and slid the case off. Then he got back on the wagon. He piled the sticks of dynamite in the center of the wagon, then wedged kegs of nails and rolls of barbed wire around them, leaving a space through which the dynamite could be seen.

Now all he had to do was drive the wagon into the

middle of the street and get away from it without getting filled with lead.

He looked over at Clint, who nodded his approval and pointed to his own gun. It was clear that Pat's job was to get the wagon into position, and then Clint would take it from there.

Pat climbed onto the seat of the buckboard and, ignoring the pain in his left arm, fixed the hitching on the wagon so that the team could be unhitched in an instant.

Now he was set, and if he didn't get blown up, catch a bullet or get dragged to death, he just might come out of this whole mess alive.

FORTY-ONE

Willy Chambers saw what Pat Garrett was doing, but couldn't figure out why. Was he going to make a run for it with the buckboard? Was he running out on Adams?

Willy had located all of his men, and now realized that his brother Seth lay dead in the street. All of his men were trained to key on him, and when they saw him rush, they'd rush.

The time to rush them was only moments away.

Garrett was throwing materials off the wagon now, probably to make it lighter. He was, however, piling nail kegs up, probably to use as cover. When Garrett started the buckboard going, Will Chambers and his men were going to rush the Gunsmith, and to hell with John Stud. After they killed Adams, he just might kill Stud as well. Willy was perfectly willing to let Garrett go as far away as he wanted with the buckboard. Once he was gone and Adams was dead, the town of Lancaster was dead.

Clint fervently hoped that he and Pat Garrett were thinking exactly alike, because any variation could prove to be fatal. It wouldn't be long before Chambers would decide to rush them, and it was doubtful that they could survive a nine-man rush.

He watched Pat with great interest, and saw that, so far, he was making all of the right moves. It was also obvious that the wound in his left arm was taking a lot out of the young lawman, and Clint hoped that he could hang on long enough to make the plan work.

Clint reloaded carefully, although he hoped to only need one shot to accomplish his aim.

Holding his gun at the ready, the Gunsmith waited for Pat Garrett to climb onto the seat of the buckboard and get under way. He just hoped that Pat would be far away from the wagon when the time came for him to fire.

> *The Gunsmith stood his ground, stolid and fearless, gun fully reloaded, while the craven Chambers gang—or what was left of them—hid, too frightened to either charge or flee.*

Pat Garrett heaved himself into the driver's seat of the buckboard, holding his left arm stiffly. He looped the rein around his right elbow, for he'd need his right hand to unhitch the team at the crucial moment. He felt naked with his gun in his holster, but it was necessary, for he was now a one-handed man and had enough work for four.

Using his foot to release the handbrake, Pat took a deep breath, and then urged his borrowed team forward, asking for as much speed as they could give him.

As the wagon began to move, Willy Chambers prepared to stand, as did Clint Adams. All eyes were on Pat Garrett's buckboard as he drove it down the street that had been chewed up by dynamite blasts.

As the buckboard approached the center of the

blasted area, Pat reached down with his good hand for the pin that attached the team to the buckboard. Grasping it tightly, and knowing full well that the reins were still wrapped around his right elbow, he pulled the pin out and was yanked from his seat and dragged on the ground by the runaway team.

He had done his part; now it was up to Clint Adams.

The wagon, still moving very quickly, was approaching the center of the blast area, and as it did he aimed his gun at the group of dynamite sticks that Pat had carefully placed in the center of the nail kegs and barbed wire. Sheriff Garrett had left the Gunsmith a very small space with which to work, but as Clint squeezed off a single shot, he knew that the bullet would travel true and strike his target—and it did.

At the moment that Pat Garrett was yanked from his seat, Willy Chambers stood up and motioned to his men to follow him. The remaining members of the Chambers gang all left their cover and charged forward toward Clint Adams, and when the bullet fired by the Gunsmith struck the dynamite sticks, all hell broke loose!

FORTY-TWO

As the dynamite exploded, everything that was packed around it went flying outward: Nails, pieces of barbed wire, chunks of wood flew in all directions, cutting, slicing and gouging, leaving in their wake bloody chunks of meat where once stood men.

Ignoring the havoc around him, Clint left his cover and went running down the street after Pat Garrett, who had all of his concern at that moment.

The young lawman had actually been dragged beyond the town limits and when Clint reached him was just trying to get to his feet.

"Pat!"

As the Gunsmith reached his young friend, Pat staggered and started to fall. Clint grabbed him and held him upright, examining him with great concern. Both of Pat Garrett's arms hung at his sides uselessly as Clint supported him—not without some difficulty due to the other's size.

"Pat, are you all right?"

"Except for my arms," he answered.

"Either one broken?"

"I don't think so," Pat answered. "I don't know. I can't move either one very well." Pat Garrett looked at Clint Adams then as if just realizing that he was there and asked, "What happened?"

"It worked, Pat," Clint replied. "There's nothing left of the Chambers gang." Tightening his grip on the big man Clint said, "Now come on, let's get you to a doctor, quick."

They turned and started walking back to town together.

Bodies littered the streets, some ripped to shreds and totally bereft of life, others still moving, only just barely. There were a few men rolling around on the ground, trying to hold together limbs, actually crying and screaming in pain.

"My God," Pat said, staring in horror and amazement.

"I know," Clint said. "I know, kid, but there wasn't any other way, believe me."

They passed the body of a man who no longer had a face and Clint fervently hoped that the man was dead.

"No other way," he repeated, as if trying to convince himself.

"Adams!" a man's voice called, and Clint froze in his tracks. He was standing with both arms around Pat Garrett, supporting him, and knew that they were both in bad trouble.

"Turn this way, Adams," the voice said. It was coming from Clint's right, and he turned that way with his burden.

The man who was speaking looked like death itself. His face and clothes were covered with blood, and the flesh that showed was torn, some pieces even hanging from the man's torso and face in flaps.

"They're all dead, Adams," he said. "My brothers, they're all dead."

"You're Willy Chambers?" Clint asked.

"That's right, Mr. Gunsmith," the man said. Clint

noticed that the man's left arm was hanging uselessly at his side, while his right hand held his weapon, pointed at Clint and Pat Garrett.

"My men and my brothers are dead, but I'm still alive, and ready to make you pay."

"Let me put my friend down and I'll be glad to oblige you," Clint said.

"Not that way, friend," Chambers said. "It's not going to be that way. You stand just as you are. First I'm going to put your friend out of his misery, and while you're holding up his dead body I'm going to pick you apart, and then put my last bullet through your head."

Christ, Clint thought. *Where the hell are Laura and Charlie Anderson now that I need them? Maybe they're both dead too, like young Billy Gaines.*

As he and Pat Garrett would be in a matter of seconds.

"Chambers," a new voice called out.

Willy Chambers turned his head in the direction of that voice and Clint wondered if he could drop Pat, draw and fire before Chambers looked back at him.

"Who's that?"

"Me, Willy," John Stud said, walking down the center of the street towards them. Looking around, Stud shook his head and said, "Jesus, what a mess."

"Stud, you son of a bitch!" Chambers hissed. He forgot about Pat Garrett and Clint Adams and moved his gun towards Stud. "You goddamn son of a bitch, you led us into this!"

"Hey, Willy," Stud said, spreading his hands. "Everybody's entitled to a mistake." Inclining his head towards the Gunsmith he added, "Besides, he just outmaneuvered us, that's all."

"My brothers are dead, you son of a bitch!" Chambers shouted. Clint saw Chambers cock the hammer of his gun, but before he could move his eyes to Stud, the gunman had already fired. His bullet struck Chambers in the center of the chest, drove him back a few steps, and then dropped him to the ground, just as dead as his brothers.

When Clint looked at Stud the man's gun was already back in his holster.

"Just thought I'd put him out of his misery," Stud said.

"And what about us?"

"I don't much care about your friend, there," Stud said, "but you and I have an appointment, right here and right now."

"Can I put him down?"

Stud shrugged and said, "What's one more body lying in the street, more or less?"

"Yeah," Clint said. "Come on, Pat. You're going to sit down for a couple of seconds."

Pat didn't answer, and when Clint looked at his face he doubted very much that his friend knew what was going on.

"Just a few minutes, that's all," Clint said, lowering Pat to the ground.

"Jesus, but you sure did a job on these men," Stud commented as Clint lowered his burden as gently as he could to the ground. "I don't think there's enough pieces left here to make up one whole man."

Clint kept his eyes on Stud while he disengaged himself from Pat Garrett, just in case of any treachery.

"Hey, don't worry," Stud said, when he recognized the Gunsmith's concern. "It don't mean a thing if it ain't fair."

"If you were a smarter man, Stud," Clint said, straightening up, "you'd know that it doesn't mean anything at all, no matter how it's done."

"You believe that, friend," Stud replied. "Maybe it'll make your grave more comfortable."

FORTY-THREE

As The Gunsmith stood amidst the bodies of the Chambers gang, all of whom had bowed to the might of his gun, he was approached and challenged by a lone gunman, a man of some repute who had the audacity to think himself the match of the infamous Gunsmith. Clint Adams calmly accepted the man's challenge, undaunted by the fact that his gun would claim one more death that day. This one, however, was the most important, for this man did not only threaten The Gunsmith's life, but his reputation, as well.

"You've got quite a reputation, Stud," Clint said, moving laterally to put some space between himself and Pat Garrett. "Why do you want to try and add mine to it?"

"With the death of Hickok, Adams, you've got the top rep with a gun," Stud explained. "I want top rep."

"You've got it," Clint said. "Take it with my blessing."

"Not that way," John Stud said, shaking his head. "I wouldn't be earning it if you just gave it to me. I'm sorry, Adams, but I've got to take it, and that means killing you."

"Enough men have died today, Stud," Clint said. "Don't make me add one more to the list."

"That's enough talk, Adams. Let's do it and get it over with."

Clint sighed and, gesturing with his left hand, said, "The first move is yours."

"First or last, it don't make a difference," Stud said.

Clint watched for Stud's move, and even as he watched he realized how dog tired he was. The man's hand flashed towards his gun and Clint actually had to shake himself to wake himself up.

He drew and fired in one smooth, fluid motion and as the bullet struck Stud's chest—just as Stud's had impacted on Chambers's chest—Stud's face reflected the shock and surprise he was feeling.

"Top rep," he said, and then a torrent of blood rushed from his mouth and he fell on his face in the sand.

FORTY-FOUR

A dozen hands from the Millar ranch galloped into town an hour after the last shot was fired. They were given the grisly task of cleaning up and burying.

Neither of Pat Garrett's arms was broken. The left one had a hole through it, and the right one had been dislocated at the shoulder. The town doctor treated both and said the sheriff would be good as new before long. Until that time, however, he would have to wear both arms in a sling, and Clint agreed to stay around long enough for at least one to be freed.

Laura Dean had been shot in the shoulder, a wound which would keep her restricted to her bed for a few days. Charlie Anderson had chosen an inopportune moment to peer over the side of his roof, and when the buckboard exploded he'd been beaned by a chunk of wood, which knocked him unconscious. He would have a headache for a couple of days, but other than that he was fine.

Billy Gaines was dead, and Cora Beth seemed very upset that he'd go and do something so inconsiderate to her. The last thing that Laura Dean did before retiring to her bed for some rest was evict Cora Beth. Clint had little doubt that she'd have no trouble finding a place to sleep—though he was certainly not one of the choices.

A few days later, the store owners who had sustained damages—not to mention the owner of the buckboard with all of the supplies it carried—lodged complaints with the town council and Mayor Gault, and insisted that the town owed them for damages caused by the actions of the sheriff.

When informed of this by Mayor Gault, while sitting in the old gentleman's office, Pat Garrett's mouth dropped open and he was at a total loss for words.

Clint looked at Pat and said, "The next thing he's going to tell you is that the amount of the damages will have to be deducted from your salary."

"What?" Pat snapped.

"Well," drawled the mayor.

"That's okay," Clint said. "Pat, why don't you go and take care of your arms? I'll handle this for you—in an unoffical capacity, of course," he added, looking at Mayor Gault.

"But—" Pat started.

"This is the last lesson, Pat," Clint said, cutting him off.

Garrett looked from Gault to Clint, and then shrugged and stood up. The big man presented an odd, almost comical figure standing there with both arms in slings, but there was nothing comical about what the mayor and the town council were trying to do to him.

"I'll see you later," Clint told him, and then he waited until the young lawman had left the office before speaking to the mayor.

"That man almost lost both arms protecting this asshole of a town, Mayor," he said tightly. "Don't you think you owe him something more than a cut in salary?"

"Business is business, Mr. Adams," Gault said.

"Speaking of which, I have a business proposition for you."

Clint hesitated a moment, then said, "Do you?"

"Yes. May I outline it for you?"

"Please, do."

Gault looked at Clint in surprise, because he thought the Gunsmith knew what he had in mind, and was surprised that he didn't reject it out of hand. "I was out on the street during the whole sordid business the other day," Gault said.

"At a discreet distance, of course," Clint added.

"Uh, yes, of course. I was observing you—"

"For one of those dime novels you write?"

"Yes. I mentioned that when I first met you, didn't I?"

"Yes, you did, but we never discussed it."

"You refused to." Suddenly, Gault narrowed his eyes and stared at Clint. "Why are you willing to discuss it now? Do you want to do a deal?"

"What kind of a deal?"

"You agree to let me do a book about you, and the town won't subtract damages from the sheriff's salary."

"You can get the council and the merchants to go for that?"

Gault smiled and said, "I can get them to go for anything I want. What do you say?" When Clint hesitated the little mayor misinterpreted the reasons and said, "I have some notes right here that I wrote that same day."

Gault waved the pieces of paper covered with his scrawl and Clint said, "May I see them?"

"Certainly," Gault said, handing them over.

Clint read the short passages that supposedly described his confrontation and single-handed destruction of the Chambers gang, then handed them back to Gault and said, "You're a writer, there's no doubt about that."

The mayor looked pleased.

"In fact, you're probably almost as good as the blackhearted bastard who first christened me the Gunsmith almost twenty years ago."

Gault's smile slipped and he did not look quite as pleased. "I don't, uh, understand."

"If you want to do a book about me, Mayor, there's something you should know."

"What's that?"

Breaking a longtime rule of never taking his gun from his holster unless he intended to use it, Clint drew his gun and rested his hand on the mayor's desk. Gault could not take his eyes off the gun, which was not even pointed at him.

"I never, never take my gun out of my holster unless I'm prepared to use it," the Gunsmith said coldly.

"I, uh, see—"

"There will be no money taken out of Pat Garrett's salary, for damages or anything else."

"I—uh, of course not," Gault said, still staring at the gun.

"And that young man will be sheriff of this pisshole of a town for as long as he likes."

"I'd, uh, have to fix elections—"

"It wouldn't be the first time, would it?"

"Uh, no, of course not."

"Good. Then we understand each other?"

"Uh, yes, we do, perfectly."

"Good."

Clint stood up and very slowly and deliberately

holstered his gun, feeling more like a fool than anything else.

"So," Mayor Gault said, also standing up, "we have a deal, then?"

"A deal?"

"Yes," Gault said. "I can write your story now."

"Which story is that?"

"This one," Gault said, touching his notes. "The one about you and the Chambers gang."

"Mayor," Clint said, "if you write that story, or any other story about me, I'll come back."

"Come back?"

"The last thing in the world I'd want to do is come back to this dunghole of a town, Mayor," Clint said, "but if I read one word about the Gunsmith, I'll come back. Understand?"

"I—understand . . . perfectly."

"Of course," Clint said, opening the door, "you'll hold up your end of the deal."

"Of course," Gault said. "Sheriff Pat Garrett won't be penalized a cent."

"Fine. It was nice doing business with you, Mayor."

When the Gunsmith left his office, Mayor Gault sat down at his desk and looked over his notes. So he couldn't do the Gunsmith story, the *Clint Adams, Town Saver* story. He still had enough here to do a nice little book of fiction. Just change the names, and the title.

High Noon at Lancaster—that was perfect.

Just perfect.

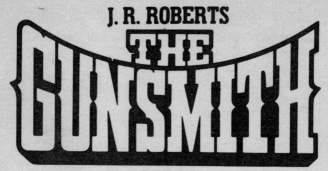

J. R. ROBERTS
THE GUNSMITH

SERIES

☐	30856-2	THE GUNSMITH #1: MACKLIN'S WOMEN	$2.25
☐	30857-0	THE GUNSMITH #2: THE CHINESE GUNMEN	$2.25
☐	30858-9	THE GUNSMITH #3: THE WOMAN HUNT	$2.25
☐	30859-7	THE GUNSMITH #4: THE GUNS OF ABILENE	$2.25
☐	30860-0	THE GUNSMITH #5: THREE GUNS FOR GLORY	$2.25
☐	30861-9	THE GUNSMITH #6: LEADTOWN	$2.25
☐	30862-7	THE GUNSMITH #7: THE LONGHORN WAR	$2.25
☐	30863-5	THE GUNSMITH #8: QUANAH'S REVENGE	$2.25
☐	30864-3	THE GUNSMITH #9: HEAVYWEIGHT GUN	$2.25
☐	30865-1	THE GUNSMITH #10: NEW ORLEANS FIRE	$2.25
☐	30866-X	THE GUNSMITH #11: ONE-HANDED GUN	$2.25
☐	30867-8	THE GUNSMITH #12: THE CANADIAN PAYROLL	$2.25
☐	30868-6	THE GUNSMITH #13: DRAW TO AN INSIDE DEATH	$2.25
☐	30869-4	THE GUNSMITH #14: DEAD MAN'S HAND	$2.25
☐	30872-4	THE GUNSMITH #15: BANDIT GOLD	$2.25
☐	30886-4	THE GUNSMITH #16: BUCKSKINS AND SIX-GUNS	$2.25

Available at your local bookstore or return this form to:

 CHARTER BOOKS
Book Mailing Service
P.O. Box 690, Rockville Centre, NY 11571

Please send me the titles checked above. I enclose
include $1.00 for postage and handling if one book is ordered; 50¢ per book for
two or more. California, Illinois, New York and Tennessee residents please add
sales tax.

NAME _____

ADDRESS _____

CITY _____ STATE/ZIP _____

(allow six weeks for delivery)

A1